WHITE KNIGHT

CD REISS

WHITE KNIGHT

PART I

CHAPTER 1

CHRIS - PRESENT

*W*hen I came to New York thirteen years earlier, I'd had ambition and seven hundred and forty-nine dollars to my name. My mother had tried to give me the last of what she had—a hundred forty dollars and some collector's coins—but I wouldn't take it. So by New York standards, I had nothing, which was easy to turn into three simple words years later from the back seat of a Porsche Cayenne.

I never glorified the first year. It sucked. They locked dumpsters at night. That was my biggest hardship. Locked dumpsters. Second only to not having money to take care of Lance.

Grappling for survival wears on a guy. It becomes the brain's primary function. I don't know how long it takes the average person before survival starts overriding more entertaining affairs, like the love of your life or happiness. In movies, soldiers are always in the trenches, looking at pictures of their girlfriends. I'd kept a picture of Catherine in my pocket. It turned into a ball the size of an aspirin when I woke up in a puddle.

Her picture was gone, but my one singular goal did not change.

Money.

I cut flowers in the backs of grocery stores. Worked construction. Learned to speak Spanish so I could get leads on new jobs. Finally I could afford a bike so I could courier documents and building plans.

Then Brian Cober's dog bit Lance's tail. *The* Brian Cober of Cober Trading Associates. Meanwhile, I couldn't afford a vet. I had no power. No leverage. Nothing. I was in that dog run every morning to develop a relationship with him, not to get into a conflict. Everyone on the Street knew Cober was a cold-eyed shark who hated to lose. What they didn't know, and I came to learn, was that he had guilt where his conscience should have been.

A conscience is a guide for living. Guilt can be bought off for a few bucks. Cober paid the vet bills and had me come in to try for a job as a runner on the floor of the Exchange. The interview was his payment. I was eager and humble. I got the job because that room and I were a match made in heaven. It reeked of what I wanted most.

Yes. Money.

I'd needed it to go back to Catherine. A lot of it. More than I could acquire without selling her memory. Earl Barrington money.

That had been thirteen years ago. Though the memory of her had faded into colorless snapshots taken by an innocent boy who no longer existed, the hunger for money hadn't.

Years after I stopped writing her letters, she became the girl I dreamed about sometimes. Or remembered when I caught the scent of roses from a flower cart. I wondered about her from my box at the US Open, when the *pop-popping* of tennis balls brought Doverton back to me.

I checked her address when I bought my co-op on Central Park South, and again when I bought the place in the Le Marais.

She still lived in the Barrington mansion, and she still had the same name.

I checked once before I married Lucia, my future wife's lipstick still smeared on my cock under my tux.

Why didn't I call her? Why just send one last envelope with a check inside a card? Why not pick up the phone?

I told myself she didn't want me, but the fact was, I was greedy. I was shallow. I was a shell of a man. I was a robot working eighty hours a week because… foreign markets, and money, money, money.

Which was about to change.

Ten years after his dog bit mine in the park, Brian knew it and I knew it.

The quants had gotten it wrong. The algo had found a trend and labeled it an outlier. I'd been outmaneuvered, and I was about to be the manager of an empty shell of a hedge fund.

A hedge fund's only capital was its reputation, and ours had taken a beating. It would take years to claw back to the top. I didn't know if I had it in me anymore.

Nella, my hipster dog walker from Brooklyn, called as I was assessing my nonexistent options. "Mr. Carmichael?"

"What?" I was annoyed. I'd hired her so I didn't have to be bothered while I was working, and there she was…

"Lance doesn't look good. He won't get up."

"What do you mean he won't get up?"

"He's awake, but he can't move. I think he needs to go to the vet."

By the time I got back to my co-op, it was too late.

In Barrington, the factory town where I grew up, when your dog died on the couch, you got your friends up to Wild Horse Hill and you all buried the body. But what did you do in New York City?

You sat on the arm of the sofa. You watched his body's stillness pour over the upholstery like a stain, covering the cushions, the furniture, the floor, and you, bruising the space with death and rigidity. It soaked everything. Color. Air. Muscle. Spirit. Emotion. The grip of the present seized time and perception, as the tunnels of future and past twisted closed and stranded me inside a hard candy shell.

And then I snapped out of it.

Past and future opened and I saw my life with new clarity. I put my hand on Lance's fur and knew he wasn't there.

"Good travels for a good boy."

I was alone.

I covered him with a cashmere throw and called the vet, who arranged for someone to come for him.

Grief wasn't a stranger. I'd lost my mother a few years earlier. My sadness then had been mitigated by the fact that in her last years, I'd been able to give her the life she'd always deserved. But Lance? Why did that sting more? Why did I feel as though he'd taken my identity with him?

My phone buzzed. It was one of the quants. I didn't want to talk about failed arbitrage timing.

Then Brian buzzed. He'd want to talk about survival strategies.

I'd bought this co-op because there was a dog run around the corner.

A text from Nella. *Barron's* wanted an interview. They'd photograph me in soft focus and pretend to have sympathy for my bad bets.

Ignoring all of it, I called Lucia.

"I heard, darling," she said with an Italian accent I used to enjoy. "I'm so sorry."

8

God, six words in and I could tell what a mistake this call was. She was talking about the fund crashing, and she had my money on her mind.

"Don't worry about your payments," I said. "They're in a separate fund."

"I'm not worried. You're a good man."

By "good man," she meant I took care of business. She meant I was responsible. But it was too close to "good boy" and Lance's body was still on my couch, an inflexible mass under a cashmere blanket.

I went into my home office. It was far away from the living room and it was all hard lines and impersonal touches.

"Christopher? Are you there?"

In the last five years, she was the only person I'd been close to, but she didn't need to know this. No one needed to know. As soon as people knew, it became real. But there it was. In the tension between my foolish need to tell someone and a more foolish need to pretend my best friend was still in the house, I said it.

"Lance died."

"Ah, I'm sorry, Christopher."

"Yeah. Bad week." An old checkbook sat on the spotless glass top of my desk. I flipped the pages of carbons absently.

"Will you have a service?" Lucia asked. "You can have something at the armory. Everyone will come."

She'd come because it would be a social event, and I'd already heard she was interviewing rich men for my old position. In normal circles, this was called "dating." I'd learned her priorities too late, and as much as they were my priorities, they disgusted me.

Money.

Maybe the fact that we shared a mutual love of money for its own sake was why I'd been suddenly repelled by her.

"No service. Not here. I just…" I just wanted to get her off the phone. "You lived with him for years. I thought you might want to know."

"Well, thank you for telling me. Will you be at the gala tonight?"

"No. Someone just came in. I have to go."

We hung up. No one had come in, of course. I lived alone.

I started a text message…

Brian—

…THEN STOPPED.

I had nothing, which meant nothing was holding me here. New York was fine, but it wasn't home. Both Lance and I were from a little town one hundred twenty miles outside of nowhere.

Lance… my last connection to Barrington was gone. Had a lifeline been cut? Or an umbilical cord I didn't need?

I'd been one kind of boy and another kind of man. I had been poor then and was disgraced now. The connections had atrophied a long time ago.

But that wasn't true. Lance had tethered me to the boy I'd been and to the woman I'd loved. With him gone, was I still linked? Or was I stranded with no family, no attachments, no one to hurt if things went south? Loneliness hung off my ribs like a lantern. This co-op. My properties. The portfolio. Built before I'd met my ex-wife, to offer security to a woman who didn't want me, and crashing with nothing to hold it up.

I needed time to sort it out but gave myself none.

Brian—I'll sell if you want it.

I TAPPED out an email quickly but didn't send it. Then I spent ten minutes looking for pen and paper.

Dear Catherine,
I will try to keep this letter short in the hope that you even remember me.

CHAPTER 2

CATHERINE - PRESENT

*T*he black garbage bag snagged on a piece of metal in the floor and ripped open, dumping a pile of unidentifiable debris all over the concrete.

I wanted to cry, but I didn't want half the town to see it.

"Let me help you." Reggie, his sandy-copper hair darkened to brown with sweat, snapped up a snow shovel that leaned against the wall. He trotted across the abandoned factory floor like a kid asking to clear my walk two months early.

"Thank you," I said, going to the long steel table in the center of the room where the roll of bags was kept. "I think we're making a dent."

The snow shovel scraped along the floor with the shriek of metal on stone, but against the backdrop of dozens of people cleaning out the space, it was barely a whisper.

"Getting that graffiti off made all the difference."

Of course he'd say that. He'd used the walls of the shuttered factory as a canvas through his early twenties, when he was as angry as the rest of the town over the closure.

The anger was still there, but a measure of the despair was being replaced with hope. The people of Barrington were working together to clean the bottling factory that had been the town's lifeblood until it closed eleven years before. The bank had repossessed the property soon after my father died and my mother defaulted on the mortgage.

Last week, a real estate agent one town over mentioned to a bartender that she was showing the factory to a Silicon Valley tycoon. The news took thirty-six hours to get to my ears. It wasn't long before the town of Barrington gathered the will to make a plan.

We needed to make the best impression. We were proud people, and that factory, my father's old factory, had been the source of that pride. I still had most of the interior keys, and the gates had been breached hundreds of times in eleven years. Only this time, we wouldn't go in to vandalize it, but to clean it.

I wouldn't see a dime from the factory's sale, but the new jobs, new people, new money would do something greater than line my pockets. It would fulfill my life's work of getting Barrington back on its feet.

Reggie scooped up a pile of junk left by teenagers and homeless adults and let it slide into the bag I held open. We filled it, tied the top, and dragged it to the open window. Florencio was by the dumpster underneath, picking up the bits of garbage around it.

"Look out below!" Reggie cried.

Florencio stepped away and we threw the bag out the window and into the dumpster with a muted crash.

It occurred to me that this was all over.

This run of despair was over. The never-ending troubles, the broken system, the exodus from a place I love—over. My trust fund had been drained, my furniture sold, my future pawned so I could keep Barrington and its people above water.

I was almost done.

That night, I cried myself to sleep as I often did. For the first time, it wasn't out of tension or habit, but fear.

CHAPTER 3

CATHERINE - SIXTEENTH SUMMER

*A*t the Doverton Country Club, a boy, *the* boy, the one who was mine the minute I saw him, worked on the grounds. He had sun-coppered hair and strong arms. In the summer, his skin was a burnished russet that made his blue eyes otherworldly. By the second week of my sixteenth summer, all the girls at the club giggled over him. They were mostly from Doverton, but he and I were from neighboring Barrington. The town bore my name because my father and his father before him had owned the bottling plant, and that was what you did back then. If you created the town and made it thrive, you named it after yourself. Fifty years later, it was still named Barrington, we still lived there, and the folks in Doverton called it Trashington.

The town's reputation bothered my father a little... but my mother? When she heard some of the Doverton Ladies of the Court hadn't invited her to a cocktail brunch because she lived *over there*, it drove her over the edge.

"Don't you give them a reason to call you trash." She sat across from us in the limo.

Harper and I got dressed in our whites once a week for tennis lessons and once again in jeans for equestrian. Dad worked at the plant, and Mom didn't drive.

"That's the first thing." She pointed at Harper. "When you hit them with your racquet, that's exactly what you're doing. Giving them a reason to look down on you because you're a Barrington."

"I didn't—" Harper's defense was irrelevant.

"If they only knew we could buy and sell all of them."

"She didn't call me trash. She said the topspin reduced the travel distance when in fact the spin vector—"

"Harper!" Mom cut her off again. "No one wants to hear a lady talk nonsense."

I wasn't thinking of my sister or how she must have felt when Mom said stuff like that, which she always did. I was thinking of myself and how I was so much more of a lady than my little sister.

"Look!" Harper pointed out the window. "There's that guy again!"

I slid over to her, and there he was. The boy with the rippling tan skin who worked the grounds, biking up the hill in his shorts and backpack. No helmet, bronze hair flapping away from his sweaty face.

His name was Chris. He had a ready smile and full lips that I knew tasted of salt and cola.

Mom *tsked*. "That boy. He's going to get himself killed. I don't know how his parents allow him to take a *bicycle* twenty-two miles to the club."

"We should give him a ride!" Harper exclaimed, eyes wide with a brilliant idea.

"Heavens, no!"

"He only has a mother," I said. I saw him in town sometimes. Marsha had told me all about him. He was our age. Trailer trash. Invisible.

As we passed him, he waved.

Harper opened the window and cupped her hands around her mouth. "Use a lower gear uphill! It increases gain ratio!"

"Thank you!" he said with a smile and flicked his gear changer.

I got away from the window as Mom took Harper by the shoulder and pulled her to her side. The driver closed and locked the window. We rode the rest of the way in silence.

CHAPTER 4

CATHERINE - PRESENT

*U*pstairs, the bed creaked.

My little sister had set it up so the stairs to her attic room didn't make a sound. She didn't want to disturb me when she came down to the kitchen late at night. But though the stairs were silent, the bed made noise when she and Taylor were... busy. The day before was the first time I heard them at it.

I was in the living room on a folding chair, sewing a button on one of her yellow polo shirts. My fingers had gone numb. I thought it was a late ache from cleaning the factory two days earlier, but in the time it took my brain to catch up with my glands, I knew it was something else. My hands had lost feeling because every bit of tactile sensation went between my legs.

It was like getting slapped awake. I froze in that chair with the needle in one hand and the bag of yellow buttons in the other.

This was my sister and a man I barely knew, but my body didn't care who they were. It recognized the rhythms of their love-making and opened me, squeezing the breath out of my lungs and making my fingertips cold.

After putting the shirt and sewing supplies on the floor next to me, I went to the front door to get some air. The house was massive but had no rugs or wall hangings. We had very little furniture. Guests sat on folding chairs and plastic outdoor furniture that had been discarded by someone else. Our father had passed seven years before, and our mother had left with a man soon after. They'd left behind a dying town and a closed factory, so I'd sold the contents of the house to help the people in the town recover. They never did, but I employed whomever I could and sold most of what we had.

Harper went along with it because she didn't care about the furniture, but she didn't agree with my strategy. She was about "maintenance." I had no idea what she was trying to maintain.

Out on the porch, the sounds of the squeaking bed faded. I took a deep breath. The house was set back on the end of a long drive, hidden from the main road by high hedges and a long garden. Overhead, birds flew south in crooked Vs and Ws. I was alone. Finally.

But the throb between my legs didn't go away. I was going to have to walk it off.

Heading down the path toward the hedges, I thought about everything except the tempo of the creaking bed. I thought of how we used to have a staff to walk down the drive for the mail, and how, before his route doubled in size, Willy would come all the way down the drive to deliver it, just for the chance to say good morning to my mother. How many people could I hire to repave it? How many children could I feed with that small job?

I'd thought the driveway repair through before, but the money always found something more important to do. I was running out of things to sell, except the house itself. No one could afford to buy it, and those who could didn't want it. So the Barrington Mansion stayed the Barrington Mansion even though it looked like no more than a big, old confection of a Victorian.

I got to the mailbox, a green-painted cast-iron chest with a bronze slot, just as Willy drove up in the white truck.

"Morning, Miss Barrington!" His seat was on the right, like a boxy, doorless European sportster. He handed me a short pile of mail.

"Morning, Willy. How's Lara doing?"

"On the mend. It itches under the cast though. She complains like she's dying of it."

"That'll be the last time she jumps off Crone's Tree."

"Probably not. You know kids. So what's happening with that boy from California? Word is he's been hanging around Miss Harper."

My body was reminded of the bed creaking. I looked away from Willy in case the feeling was all over my face. "I think he's all right."

"How long's he staying?"

The town was very protective of Harper and me, even though we were adults. My father's dying wish was that they take care of us, and when folks here agreed, it was a solemn oath.

"Long enough for her to break his heart, I'm sure."

Willy laughed and waved. He pulled onto the road, and I flipped through my mail as I walked back to the house. A few bills. Marketing junk. An early birthday card for me.

When I got to the white business-sized envelope with my name in dark blue ball point, I stopped. Stood in place. It was an expensive buff paper. The return address was engraved in slate grey.

Him.

I hadn't heard from him since the night he left me.

Not a word.

And now… today.

All the other envelopes slipped to the ground, abandoned like old lovers.

Dear Catherine of the Roses,
I will try to keep this letter short in the hope that you even remember me. I'm
not used to writing things by hand, but I thought you deserved the effort.
Lance has died. He was an old dog and he had a good life, but now I have to
bring him home.
I will be burying him on Wild Horse Hill. The service is set for next Friday.
You aren't obligated to come, but I would very much like to see you while
I'm there.
Christopher

I READ IT AGAIN.

...you deserved the effort...

DID I SUDDENLY DESERVE EFFORT?

...Lance has died...

OH, terrible. Terrible. Such a sweet dog, waiting patiently for us at
the base of the tree.

...next Friday...

THE DAY after my twenty-ninth birthday. So many years.

21

…You aren't obligated…

How far down the path had we come to have no obligations?

…while I'm there…

While he's here.

…I'm there…

He's coming here.

…Christopher.

Christopher.

CHAPTER 5

CHRIS - PRESENT

*I*t was my shop, which meant I could come and go as I pleased. But it was my shop, which meant my absence was noticed.

"You're not going to Catalina." Brian sat on the other side of my desk, slouched in the leather-and-chrome chair with an ankle over his knee. He was twelve years older than me, but while I wore suits, he was a Henley-and-jeans guy. He weaponized casual. Nothing showed you were too good for all this shit like sneakers. "You're not going to Martha's Vineyard, the house on Lake Como, or the Reykjavik retreat. What am I supposed to think?"

"What you think is up to you. What you're *not* supposed to think is that I'm making side deals."

"Why shouldn't I?"

"Because you trust me."

"This might be a bad time, don't you think?" He tapped his thumbs together, the only indication that anything serious was happening. "We're in the middle of a crisis. Our investors are concerned."

"They knew the risks."

23

"That's going to go over like double-dipping in the latrine."

"What does that even mean?"

"'You knew the risks' isn't a way to do business if you want to continue doing business."

"I'm not going to continue doing business. I overleveraged." I pressed my hands to the desk glass. "I had a good run, but it's over. If you want it, make an offer."

He smirked. "You're so young." He leaned forward, putting his hand out to stop my objections. "It's fine. That was always your selling point. No one wants an old genius. But listen. You've never dealt with the ups and downs. Shit crashes. You pick up the pieces. It's not that big a deal."

"It's a big deal." I picked up my bag and slung it over my shoulder. Having started out as a bike courier, I never got over the easy weight distribution of a messenger bag. No one on the street used briefcases anymore anyway. "I don't know if I'm hungry enough to drag the fund out of the gutter."

He leaned back into his relaxed dude posture. "It's in your blood. If you're not hungry, you're not Chris Carmichael."

"Maybe." I left room for the fact that he could be right, but I wished I didn't have to. If I was nothing but a hunger, who was I when I was fed? And if there was more to me, what was it? "I have to get my head together."

"Don't take too long, kid. The market moves fast."

CHAPTER 6

CATHERINE - SIXTEENTH SUMMER

The first time I got close to Chris, I was a week into the summer after my junior year at Montgomery High. I was leaning on the court fence, waiting for my coach, and Chris was edging the grass with a Weed Whacker. I heard it and felt the pricks of cut grass on the backs of my calves. I stepped away from it.

"Sorry, miss."

"It's all right, I—"

My voice hadn't drifted off or gotten lost. I didn't swallow the rest of the sentence or forget what I was saying. The final words never existed. Everything before I saw him was fake, and after that moment, my life became real. Like Dorothy walking out of her black-and-white world into a three-dimensional colorscape.

My life wasn't divided into the years before that moment and the time after because he was handsome or strong. It wasn't because he was charming or interesting.

It was because he was mine.

We stood watching each other through the chain-link fence,

and I knew I was just as much his. We claimed each other in those first seconds.

Blue is blue and the sky is up and the earth is down. These aren't articles of faith or belief, but knowledge. Necessity. Denying gravity existed wouldn't hurt you, because it was always the law, and up was still up and down was still where you landed when you jumped.

A yellow ball bounced behind me, skidding and clicking against the fence.

"Catherine!" Dennis, my coach, called. He could hit drunk, but speaking was harder. He slurred at the ends of his sentences. He'd always said muscle memory was more powerful than anything the brain could remember. He said your body was smarter than your mind.

He was right. My body knew this young man with the blades of grass stuck to his pants and the specks of dirt on his cheeks.

"Hey, Catherine." The boy said my name like a prayer that had already been answered.

The ball rolled by my feet. I tapped it, bouncing it under my control, until I got the string face under it and I could let it roll across. Admittedly, I was being a bit of a show-off before I replied.

"Hi, Weed Whacker guy."

"I'm sorry if the noise bugs you. I can do court seven."

"You're not bothering me."

The distance between us, the fence, the next hour of lessons, all of it overwhelmed me. Too many obstacles.

He made the first move, stepping away from the fence and saluting. "Next time then."

He took his Weed Whacker to court seven, and I hit the ball back to my coach.

I never hit so hard or so accurately. I astonished Coach

Dennis, but I wasn't surprised. I was sure everything I'd do from then on out would be right and true.

When I finished my lesson, the boy with the Weed Whacker and I found each other by the water fountains, attracted like magnets. We didn't say hello or introduce each other.

Wide-eyed, he said, "Did you feel it?"

I knew exactly what he meant.

"I did. I did feel it."

We stole to the back room of the pro shop to marvel at this unnamed thing that changed everything.

"What was it?" I asked when he closed the door.

"I don't know." He touched my arm.

It felt as though two planets that had been on separate trajectories for light years had finally collided and melded. I stared at his hand, and when he tried to move it, I put mine on top of his.

"Have you felt it before?" I asked.

"No. But I still kind of... it's still there."

"Yeah. Me too. I'm..." What I was about to say had felt so trivial, I almost skipped the step. "I'm Catherine."

"I know."

Of course. In our little fishbowl, I was famous.

"I'm Chris. Chris Carmichael."

"Chris." I said his name the way he'd said mine, finally understanding how to pray for something I'd already been given. It was almost the same as praying that it not be taken away.

"I have to see you again," he said as if waking from a half-dream.

I could. I had to. I had no choice. But I couldn't agree before Irv, who ran the shop, burst in with a clipboard. He had a huge round belly, crooked teeth, and a soft spot for Barrington kids who needed jobs.

He froze when he saw us. "Carmichael, get out to court seven and finish the job." His eyes flicked to me and back to Chris.

"Yes, sir."

"And young lady?"

I held up my chin. I was an heiress and a club member.

"I believe you don't want your mother to hear back about this. So keep it quiet."

I didn't realize at the time that he was protecting Chris, but later, after I realized it, I was grateful to him.

Though in the end, no one could protect Chris but me.

CHAPTER 7

CATHERINE - PRESENT

*H*is letter was folded up in my pocket. It didn't change anything right away. It took a day or so to think of Chris with a smile on my face, and another day or so to see the conditions I lived in. The patchwork of pipes and electrical work. The bare walls and barren floors. My clothes were in good shape because Ronnie was a seamstress who could repair anything, and my hair was decent because the Snip-n-Save needed every customer they could get.

I wiped down the green tile kitchen counter, seeing every encrusted piece of grime as if for the first time. A person got used to things. A bit of grime that didn't come out on the first scrub just stayed there until new eyes saw it.

Harper flew down the stairs in the yellow polo shirt she had to wear at the Amazon distribution center where she and half the town worked, her blond hair tied into a loose ponytail.

"Hey," she said when she burst into the kitchen and opened the fridge. "Taylor's hanging out here today. You should put him to work."

"Can he do anything?"

"Yeah." She pulled out yogurt. "Surprisingly, for such a nerd."

"He didn't seem like a nerd to me." I got a bowl and a box of granola from the cabinet. "He's quite handsome and confident."

She blushed a little, taking the granola and bowl. "He's all right."

Harper was a nerd herself, spending hours in front of a computer she'd built from parts. She'd gone to MIT for a year, but came home when Daddy got sick. She never went back. Staying in Barrington was a terrible waste of her mind. A brilliant, stubborn, loyal mind.

"Do you remember Chris Carmichael?" I asked. "From the country club? He gardened for us one summer. Lived in the trailer park by the station?"

"Yeah, duh." The granola tinkled into the bowl.

"He sent me a letter." I peeled the top off the yogurt container and plucked a spoon out of the rack.

Her eyes went as wide as her bowl. "Really? What did he say?"

"Lance died." I dropped a lump of yogurt into her bowl and gave her the spoon.

"Aw," she said, poking her spoon against the bottom of the bowl. "Percy's the last of that litter."

I didn't give myself a second to doubt my next question. I just spit out what was on my mind, too late to sound casual. "I was wondering if you'd look Chris up on the computer? See how he's doing?"

She put her back to the counter and held the bowl in front of her, swirling the granola into the yogurt. "Why?"

"Because I'm asking."

"Yeah, but I don't know what you're asking for exactly? Do you want to know where he works or do you want his bank account info?"

"Harper Barrington!" I scolded. "You said you stopped that!"

She shrugged. Did I like that she was a hacker? No. But I could only make her promise she wouldn't steal or cheat. She'd never promised to stop hacking. At this point, she was a grown woman and I was so ignorant of the digital world, I didn't even know what the promise meant.

Besides, she needed to exercise her mind, not shut it down.

"I don't want his bank information," I said.

"Too bad." She ate like a prisoner of war.

"What do you mean?"

She scraped the last of the yogurt out of the curve of the bowl. "He's loaded."

My heart twisted and my skin got hot. Not because he had money. She could have revealed that he was a schoolteacher and I would have had the same reaction. My body reacted to the fact that she, my sister, anyone in the same room as me, knew anything about him. It was like touching him from a universe away.

I didn't know how much further I wanted to go, but Harper wasn't one to slip through a door quietly; she burst through.

"Has his own hedge fund and a seat on the Exchange. Ex-wife but no kids."

He'd gotten married? That seemed impossible. How could what we had be replicated in the same lifetime?

"Really?" I held up my chin. I didn't want to show her that I was tripped up.

"Italian model. I forget her name. He's got a sweet penthouse on Central Park West and a net worth around—"

"Stop!"

She obeyed, washing the bowl with a roll of her eyes. My own sister was closer to him than I was. And the ex-wife…

I had to swallow a lump of jealousy before I spoke again. "You've been talking to him?"

"Hell, no!" She put the bowl in the rack. "But I've been watching, more or less. He can't see me do it and it's mostly legal."

"Mostly?"

"I won't get caught and I don't touch anything."

"Fine, I guess." I pulled a towel off the rack and dried the bowl. "He seems all right?"

"Yeah. Kinda. Healthy, wealthy. He doesn't go out much. Just big events."

"And he's divorced?"

"Yeah. Recently. She's dumb. I can tell."

I laughed a little but not a lot. The jealousy was pushing its way back up my throat. "As long as you say so."

"Why are you asking?"

I would have to tell her at some point. The minutes before she ran out the door were as good as any. "He's coming back to bury Lance."

"Wow." She shook her head a little, staring at me as if the shock kept her from averting her gaze. "We have to clean up."

"I can manage it."

"And the thorn bush?" She indicated the backyard with a flip of her fingers. "That's not going to go over well—oh." She froze as if realizing something unpleasant. "Reg."

"I keep telling you there's nothing between Reggie and me."

"But I keep hoping."

"You're sweet. But no."

With a glance at the clock, she started out. She gave me a list of things to pick up when I went shopping, including a strange men's toiletry item. I assumed it was for Taylor, and as she drove away, I felt that little bit of jealousy well up again. My sister was performing mundane tasks for a man she cared about. I longed to do the same.

I'd dated men since he left. I'd had some sex with those men, none of it memorable. There was no love like his. I'd tried to find it and come up emptyhanded enough times to give up. I'd given up on him coming back a decade ago, given up on doing more than treading water, given up on dating.

Most days, I didn't think about him at all. Sometimes when the roses were blooming and the evening wind blew the right way, I'd remember how he made me feel, but not him in particular.

I went to the back of the house and looked at the backyard and the family cemetery. It had been there before the house, when the first Barrington Father bought land by the river and died before he'd amassed enough wealth to build on it.

When I was a girl, the plot had been lined with beautiful rose-bushes. After our father died, we'd let them grow over the head-stones that Harper had defaced when she was angry, and as the years went on, we'd let it grow into a bed of thorns. Sometimes, in the spring, they bloomed. But the bushes were too thick to be penetrated by a gardener, so they were wild and unpredictable. We just trimmed the edges so the thorns didn't go past the short white fence around the plots.

Would Chris even care?

Would he laugh or be disappointed?

I didn't know him or who he'd become, except that he was rich and lived a beautiful life. I lived with a dense thorn bush in my yard because my sister hated our father. The weight of shame I carried got denser and heavier. I could bear it inside Barrington, but in front of Chris, it would crush me.

The note crinkled in my pocket. For the first time since getting it, I thought I should tell him I wouldn't see him.

CHAPTER 8

CATHERINE - SIXTEENTH SUMMER

On Mondays, Wednesdays, and Saturdays in the summer, Mom went into Doverton to ride horses with the Princes. She showered there, and often got home smelling of soap and perfume. Otherwise, she hovered over us like a hummingbird. She had a staff of nannies and sitters assigned to watch us during the moments she turned her back, but they were no more than moments.

Behind the rose cemetery stood a narrow band of untouched forest, then high grasses, then the river. Daddy had built a bridge over the river. He walked across it to the bottling factory six days a week and stayed there fourteen hours a day.

Soon after Chris and I met at the club, he got a job with Garden Haven. He told me later that getting a job with the company who did our landscaping was part of his plan to see me.

He rode his bike to us on Fridays to prune and water. It had a trailer with his tools. Mom had seen him caring for the roses at the club and put him in charge of the bushes in the little cemetery. She didn't like being inside the fence herself, because it reminded her that she was destined to lie there for eternity.

34

"He's taking a while back there," Harper said.

We were on the screened-in back porch, under ceiling fans. It was still muggy and thick. My thighs slid against each other as I watched Chris's body bend and straighten as he worked on the roses.

Harper turned her attention back to her *Complete Works of Sir Arthur Conan Doyle*. She was reading well past her grade level. It was the only respite from her painful social awkwardness. "Twenty-two percent longer, at this point."

"It's the heat."

Our meeting in the back of the pro shop was a week old. I'd seen him twice since then. His lips tasted of salt and cola, and the young body felt tight and hard under his shirt.

Watching Chris, I wasn't completely sure if it was all sweat greasing the insides of my thighs. He'd led me behind a secret fence at the back of the club. He laid a towel over a tree stump so I wouldn't get grass or dirt stains on my white clothes, and he kneeled in front of me. When he kissed me, I wanted to spend the rest of my life attached to his lips, tasting his tongue. He'd bought me a soda, and we took turns transferring a chip of ice between our mouths.

That night, I'd run my fingers over my lips to see if I could reproduce the feeling, then between my legs for the same reason. Fear stopped me from continuing to the end. What if someone saw? What if my mother's voice in my head wasn't just a voice? What if—when it burst in saying "how *could* you?"—it summoned her attention by some as-yet-undisclosed telepathic transference and she could see me?

When Chris stood and wiped his brow, I imagined how his cola lips would taste with a hint of rose on them. He turned away as if something was moving in the trees and waved. A second later, Johnny came through the forest, holding a banker's box. His son, ten-year-old Joe, was at his side.

Johnny worked at the factory as a chemical engineer. His wife, Pat, owned the grocery store by Barrington Burgers.

Harper stood. "It's Mister Dorning! Hey, Mister Dorning!"

She was twelve and didn't have great impulse control. She had a special rapport with Johnny, based on their mutual love of things I couldn't get my head around.

Johnny stood by the white fence with his box. Chris looked into it and smiled. I didn't want him smiling without me. If I was miserable and ashamed, he had to be too. I went out, pulled behind Harper as if on a tether.

Johnny put the box on the ground, and everyone looked into it.

Harper squealed with delight. "Can I have one?"

The box was full of puppies. Four of them. The bloodhounds were honey-brown and cheerful except for the smallest one. He just looked soulful.

"It's up to your parents," Johnny said.

"I like this one!" Joe said, patting a tail-wagger with her paws over the edge of the box. She licked the boy's hand.

"Me too," Chris said.

I realized he was close to me and snapped around to see him looking over my shoulder, bent at the waist so his hands leaned on the three-foot-high fence and his lips were an inch from my body. He flicked his finger against the top of my thigh and I nearly went blind with arousal.

"I like the little one," I heard Harper say from a million miles away.

Chris and I were eye-locked. I could smell his breath, his body, the heat coming off him.

"He's the runt of the litter," Johnny said.

"What's that mean?" little Joe asked.

"He'll have certain genetic disadvantages," Johnny replied.

"In the wild," Harper corrected.

Chris blinked. Licked his lower lip. I couldn't tell if it took more effort to not kiss him or to stay standing.

"If I take him, he'll have advantages," Harper added.

The voices came from a long tunnel between my connection with Chris and the rest of the world clamoring for attention and getting none.

"We're naming them after Arthur's knights," Johnny said from the end of the tunnel.

"I read *Sir Gawain* in spring." That was Harper's voice.

Johnny. "I remember."

Little Joe. "Lancelot should be the big one! And Galahad because he's the best."

Their voices melted into the density of the silence between Chris and me like chocolate in a marble cake.

"Two are girls."

"Galahad can be shortened to Gal."

"The runt is Percival and he's mine."

"I promised the runt to Orrin. He needs a beta."

"We need an Arthur and there's no girl name for it."

"We can call a girl Arthur."

"There something wrong with Guinevere?"

I shook my head ever so slightly and pressed my lips tight together.

My expression was meant to speak a few volumes.

Not here.

I can't look at you like this here.

"Harper Barrington! You put that mutt down!"

I snapped to attention. Harper had the little puppy in her hands. Our mother bounded down the back porch steps.

Johnny gently took the dog from my sister before our mother reached us. "I'm sorry, Ella. I didn't think—"

"No, you didn't."

37

"But, Mom…" Harper whined, and Harper never whined. "He's just a baby. He needs us."

"Your father is allergic."

"We'll keep him outside."

"No. Go wash your hands."

Harper stormed off, fists balled on the ends of stiff arms, feet slamming the ground as if she wanted to bruise it.

"I'm sorry, Johnny," Mom said gently.

"I get it."

Their eyes locked, and having just had an eye-lock with Chris, I recognized the similarity. But it didn't last. Not for even a second.

She spun to me, then Chris, smoldering like hot glass. "Are you finished?"

"Not quite, ma'am."

"I'm not paying you for the time you spend looking at puppies."

"Of course." Chris pointed at Johnny and stepped back. "I'll take Lancelot."

"You got it," Johnny replied. "You sure you don't want one, El?"

My mother was kneeling over the box, letting one of the dogs lick her hand. "Earl's too sensitive." Mom stood and put her hand on my shoulder. "Let's get in out of the sun."

I followed her back to the house, looking back only once. Chris was looking at me with his arm shielding his eyes from the glare.

When we got inside, my mother guided me to the kitchen faucet, where we washed our hands. She kept looking out the back window over the sink.

"Is this clean enough?" I asked, willing my eyes away from Chris, into the endless drain.

"Yes." She shook the water off her hands. "Come here with me."

She took me to the sun room that overlooked the side of the house. It had windows on three sides and, for that moment, was remarkable for the fact that we couldn't see the backyard from it.

"Catherine," she said, folding her hands in her lap, "are you all right?"

"Yes." I pressed my knees together, wondering if she could see what was happening under my skirt.

She wiggled in her seat as if the conversation made the cushions prickly. "That boy was looking at you."

"I didn't notice."

She sighed. "Where I grew up, in Philadelphia, we were exposed to more things. More men. I worry about you girls's prospects."

I knew where she was going, and I wanted to deflect her. "I'm not worried about me. Harper though? She's so smart."

"She'll meet a man in college."

"Maybe I will too."

She nodded with the satisfaction of a period after a long string of clauses. "Boys like the one out there will ruin your life. Trust me on that. I won't let it happen. Trust me on that too." She looked me right in the eye, one eyebrow raised as if she expected me to rubber stamp her message.

I nodded slightly, because I was sure she was right. He'd ruin my life. I just had to decide if I wanted it ruined.

"Catherine." She tilted my chin up at her. "It's hard being a woman. In Philadelphia, it was hard because you were expected to do everything. Family, work, everything. Here, it's hard because you can let a man take care of you, but you can't make a mistake. There's no coming back from them. Do you understand what I'm saying?"

I didn't. Mistakes weren't always mistakes until after they happened. "Did you make a mistake once?"

"No." Her answer was sharp, as if she was cutting off a contradiction. "I married your father and he brought me here. And now I have my two girls who I love more than anything."

I wanted to make her happy. I wanted to make her proud and do things the right way. But as she hugged me, I wondered when I'd come to where the road forked between completing her life and completing my own.

CHAPTER 9

CHRIS - LAST DAYS OF LANCE

*L*ance liked everyone. He'd even liked Lucia, more or less, though she was never warm to him and she constantly complained about his hair getting in her sweaters. She'd had a point. We had a maid five days a week, yet his stiff fur always wound up in her knitwear. She gave up on wearing anything black more than once. I thought it had been Lance's way of chasing her out.

I gave him a pat on the head and tossed him a treat. He caught it, but he wasn't jumping as high as he used to or landing as confidently. He crunched it slowly, as if his teeth hurt.

I didn't think about him getting old. I thought he'd be with me forever.

He finished the treat and slapped his tail on the kitchen tile.

Fuck it. I gave him another treat and put the box away. When I lifted my arm to reach the cabinet, I caught sight of a dog hair in my sweater. And another.

"I'm going to change."

He followed me to the bedroom.

Lucia had bought me a pet hair remover brush as a divorce

present. I should have been heartbroken to even look at it, but when we split up, I wasn't hurt. I was relieved.

I never had to see Lucia again. I never had to hear her brittle, derisive laugh or be nice to her friends. I never had to pretend I was the one throwing her birthday extravaganza. I didn't have to go to another Montano Foundation event where she worked tirelessly to help children she'd never know to make up for the children she couldn't have.

In the end, it was all about money. Even if she'd ever loved me, by the end, all the love had turned into money.

So fuck me for not seeing it.

Fuck me for letting her push me into a marriage I didn't want.

Fuck me for being weak.

Lance and I wrestled around for a few minutes, but he was old and tired. He couldn't play too rough or for too long. In the end, I rolled onto my back, arms and legs spread, looking at the white ceiling.

I didn't trust people easily. Why had I fallen for her eight years ago? I had been a kid from nowhere, a little prick hotshot throwing money around in restaurants. She'd been an Italian model for fifteen minutes. She'd started a charity with millions collected from men she denied were ex-lovers. On paper, she seemed better than I could do.

Fuck the paper. Never again. She should have been no more than an aspirational fuck.

Whatever. There was no need to worry about it. I was free. I could go anywhere. I could do anything.

I took Lance by the ears and looked into his brown eyes. "You're the only one for me, ya hear?"

He licked my chin and gave me his special whine that translated to, "Go for walk."

"Okay, boy."

He leapt for the door. By the time I got there, his tail was smacking the molding and he had his leash in his teeth. I was just about to grab it when my phone rang.

"Give me a second." I checked the caller ID and answered. "Brian."

"Did you see Neville's London report? If we make the arbitrage window, there's a thirty percent return."

"Thirty?" Holy crap. That was insane.

"Guaranteed. We need to move on this now."

"And big." I'd paced back to my home office with a mind fully occupied with calculating closing times and exchange rates. We had eleven minutes.

Brian and I spoke our shorthand, moving money, calculating odds, agreeing to go big on a hunch I'd had the day before and handed to Neville for calculations. We hung up at nine minutes and I pumped the fist that held the phone with a "yes!"

A nice afternoon's work.

I came back to the front of the house whistling fucking Dixie.

Lance was whimpering, his chin on his front paws. The fur was dark and damp at the ends, and a puddle of piss spread over the floor, flowing in rivulets toward the forty-thousand-dollar Persian rug.

"Crap!"

Lance whined and gave me his guilty face, but I didn't have time. I snapped paper towels off the roll and saved the rug.

"It's all right," I said to Lance on my hands and knees. "It's my fault, but I just made a ton of money."

Lucia's voice in my mind cut through my satisfaction. "*Porque?* Christopher, what are you going to do with all this money?"

That question had come toward the end, and it baffled me. She'd loved spending my money. I'd thought she loved me, but in moments when I was honest with myself, I thought it was all about the money for her.

I squirted disinfectant on the floor and rolled off more paper towels, recalling the night I met her.

I was sure she was about the money, and I was stupid and all right with that. I liked it, because she'd have me for what I'd done, not who I was.

She'd been looking over my shoulder at Lola's. Bernie had been talking about my quant fund and she was cooing about how she didn't understand it. I'd tried to hide my phone screen because... why?

Right. I'd been looking at my checking account. Why? To prove some shit to Bernie?

Why would I call up my checking account on my phone? At dinner, no less. The most interesting transactions weren't in the checking. That was a slush fund for bills and crap.

Lucia had long nails. She'd run them along the back of my hand as I'd slid my fingers over the glass.

"You have a dog?" she asked, pulling a hair off my sleeve.

"Yeah."

"Little or big?"

She was making conversation, which you were supposed to do at a big dinner. I was agitated the night I'd met Lucia. I knew why for a while, then I forgot. Something in the checking account had been bugging me.

"Medium."

I'd been counting days.

Why? I wasn't late with anything. I had a team of people to pay the damn bills. What was it with the checking account eight years ago? And why had it mattered?

Tossing the last of the soiled paper towels, I leaned down to face my dog. "Do you still want to go out? Walk?"

Of course he did. We went around the corner. He gave what he had left to a few hydrants and I tried to pull apart that night with Lucia.

My personal checking account. *Why why why?*

When we got back, I poured Lance some water, but instead of drinking, he followed me to my office. It was hardwood and chrome, shine and windows. My weekend hideaway from the social dramas of the fashion world that Lucia brought home. Throwing open the closet doors, I rooted past the bank boxes and corporate binders on the top shelf, finding my old checkbooks.

Counting backward, I found the checks I would have written when I met Lucia. *No, no, no.* Lance plopped down in front of me and whined, tilting his head toward my desk. I didn't know if it was because of the pain in his spine or if he was trying to mention that looking at my bank account online would be easier.

"I think I'll remember better if I feel the paper, you know?" I told him.

He put his chin between his paws and watched me with his big brown eyes, as if he knew what I was about to find out.

"Something you want to tell me, boy?"

He just blinked.

"Fine." I flipped through the book.

Like most people, I used mostly online payments and bank transfers, so a carbon for a check dated six months before I met Lucia wasn't too hard to find.

Seven hundred forty-nine dollars, made out to Catherine Barrington.

My phone number was in the memo.

Yeah.

That was why I'd been looking at my checking account.

Check 3201 had never been cashed, and the night I'd met Lucia was exactly six months after it was dated. The last day it was valid.

That was the night I gave up on Catherine.

CHAPTER 10

CATHERINE - PRESENT

Dear Chris,
Your letter came as a surprise. It's wonderful to hear from you after all these
years. How they've flown by!

$\mathcal{I}$ tapped my finger against the kitchen counter, reading the note. The black ballpoint handwriting was fine. Neat as a pin. The stationary was old Barrington family paper that I kept in the bottom of my underwear drawer because I had nowhere else to put it. Everything was fine with the note except the intent.

The soup for church was popping and boiling in the pot. The dishes were clean, and I had nothing to do but write this note. I wished I had something else to do.

Your letter came as a surprise. It's wonderful to hear from you after all these
years. How they've flown by!

I sounded like a stranger. Like someone who had never

promised him a thing. Even the exclamation point at the end that was supposed to warm up the letter seemed like another line and dot of distance.

Pushing the paper's corners together, I started to crumple it and stopped. I could use it as scrap. I could write everything I wanted to say then edit it neatly onto a new sheet.

I am so sorry to hear about Lance. I think burying him at home is the right thing. I know Galahad is on Wild Horse Hill. You should get a space nearby.

Was that all I was going to talk about? Lance? Was I going to let the subtext rule the conversation or was I going to be a grown-up?

I don't know when I stopped waiting for you.

There. That was closer. At least it was true. A long time ago, I'd stopped waiting without even thinking about it.

I used to cry over you, but not for a long time. Now I just cry out of habit. I cry for a release, even if I don't feel sad. It's a valve I can open and I function fine. So, thanks for the tears, I guess.

The bedsprings squeaked upstairs, and my stream of rage snapped. This thing Harper had. This man she'd met on the

47

internet and brought home. It was strange and unprecedented and I wanted it.

I didn't even know what it was and I wanted it. I wanted it so badly I couldn't think.

To add shame to sin, the doorbell rang.

I looked through the front sidelight. It was Reggie.

"Shoot."

He worked in the distribution center off the interstate and painted small canvases of cities and spaceships in his spare time. He'd sold a few to people in Doverton, but mostly he covered them over with new ideas as they occurred.

When I was upset, my father gave me the master suite as a consolation prize. At twenty, Reggie was Barrington's resident artistic talent. Dad had hired him to paint flowers on the ceiling to cheer me up. I didn't sleep in that room anymore because of a roof leak, but knowing the ceiling was there was comforting. It was beautiful and it was mine.

My sister and every lady in town insisted Reggie held a candle for me ever since then. Even while I dated Frank Marshall and after that ended peacefully. The rumors alone put Reggie at the top of the list of people I didn't want to come inside while Taylor and Harper were making a racket.

Pressing the pedal to open the kitchen garbage pail, I gathered the top of the plastic bag. It was only about a third full, but I took it to the front door anyway. When I opened it, Reggie had his hat in his hand.

"Hello," I said.

He stuffed his baseball cap in his back pocket and took the bag. "I have that."

"Thank you." I pointed down the driveway.

The garbage pails were on the side of the house so they were easily accessed from the side door. Hopefully he'd think I came to the front to answer the doorbell, as opposed to using the garbage as an excuse to keep him out of the house and away from the sound of the bed squeaking.

He followed where I indicated without question, walking around the side with me.

"What brings you here on Sunday morning?"

"I just found out from Johnny that old Chris Carmichael's coming back."

"Really?"

"So they say."

We walked a few more steps.

"He might," I said. "But who knows?"

"Did he tell you?"

"Why would he?"

"You guys had a thing."

"That was a long time ago." I opened the garbage pail lid. "Why?"

He put the bag inside. "I was wondering how you were about it? Happy?"

"It's complicated." I let the lid slap shut. "A lot's changed. I mean, look around here. When he left, the burger place was packed every night, the factory was open, my family? We... we were big shots."

"You're still a big shot to me." He was being completely earnest. He was a trash-talking guy's guy when he thought I wasn't looking, but around me, he was warm and sincere.

"Thank you, Reg."

He cleared his throat. "So what are you going to do with that thorn bush out back? Those roses were his pride and joy."

"Hardly."

"Aw, come on. He worked twelve hours at a time on them. Pruned and mulched. I remember."

I wanted them to be nice for him, but I also didn't want to see him. I wished I could be of a single mind about anything. "I should probably make them into proper bushes again."

I walked Reggie to his car. It was the only subtle way I had of letting him know he couldn't come inside.

"If you need any help, I'm pretty handy with clippers."

"You're good at too many things, Reggie."

"I said I was handy." He flipped his hat back on. "I make no other promises."

"Will I see you at church?"

"Yes, ma'am."

"I'm making the soup everyone likes."

"I'll come hungry then."

He got into his car. We said our so longs and he drove off.

Back inside, I was glad I hadn't invited Reggie in. They were still at it. Maybe they were trying to be quiet the same way I tried to be quiet when I cried at night.

The sounds were lower by the couch. The sewing kit was on the arm because I'd sold the end tables and coffee table. The kit's lid had a hard inside surface. I opened it, put a blanket over my legs, and began my letter to Chris again.

CHAPTER 11

CATHERINE - SIXTEENTH SUMMER

*B*ehind the courts, between the locker room and the club, there was a shortcut for members and an artery for the grounds staff. Behind that was a quarter-acre patch of grass between the fence and Route 42 which stretched between Doverton and Barrington. The entire lot was visible to the road, but there was a tree in the middle of it. A mighty oak with horizontal branches thicker than most tree's fully-grown trunks.

When Chris had a minute and happened upon the right piece of wood, he'd nail chunks of two-by-four or one-by-four into the trunk. He told me about it behind the pool house and in the hidden corners of the parking lot.

I didn't know what he was talking about until he finished at mid-summer and led me through a hole in the fence. "Where are we going?"

I was barely through before Lance bounced over to me, stopping right before he came to the end of a long chain. Still a puppy, he had big brown eyes and floppy ears with short fur the color of hazelnuts. I ran my hands over his body, and he rolled onto his back.

"Is he safe here?" I asked, crouching to rub his belly.

"Pretty safe. Irv says it's okay as long as I clean up after him and he's quiet."

Lance twisted around and nipped my fingers playfully, trying to wrestle my hand.

"Where's your ball?" Chris asked.

Lance bounced back to the base of his captivity. The tree. I stood and slapped my hands clean. Chris laid his hand on the back of my neck. I shuddered.

"I was watching you play," he whispered in my ear. "Do you know you smile before forehands?"

"You should tell me when you're there."

"Next time." He nipped my earlobe, his breath loud in my ear.

Lance dropped a sticky ball at our feet. Chris knelt and patted his head, reaching into his pocket for a new yellow ball. Lance was thrilled. Chris tossed it toward the tree and the puppy ran for it. Chris took my hand and led me to the tree.

"Put your foot on this." He laid his hand on the lowest piece of wood, at knee height. "I've tried it already. It's safe."

I dropped my bag at the trunk, and he helped me balance as I got my tennis shoe on the bottom foothold. My hands found the boards above, and I stepped up. At the second step, I pressed the back of my skirt against my bare thighs and looked down at him.

"You'll need two hands to climb," he said.

Behind him, on the ground, Lance looked up at us with his tongue hanging out.

"I think you should go first," I said.

"You're wearing shorts under your skirt. I can't see a thing."

The shorts protected my bottom from view while I ran and spun on the tennis court. But they were still really short, and he was getting a longer look.

"Do you promise?"

"Swear."

I decided to believe him and climbed until I was fifteen feet off the ground, on a bough thicker than a telephone pole. I straddled the bough and slid back so Chris could fit. He straddled it facing me. Below us, Lance protected the new ball by yipping. I could hear cars on Route 42 and the *pock pock* of tennis balls hitting the court, but all I could see were leaves, branches, and mottled sunlight.

"Do you like it?" he asked.

"I love it."

He licked his finger and chalked one up for himself. "Did you decide about college next year?"

I shrugged. I wanted to get out of Barrington. Spread my wings. Meet new people and learn new things. But Chris couldn't afford to go to college.

"Did you check out the financial aid booklet at the library?" I asked.

"There's no point."

"Well then, I'll get an Associate's from Jackson County. I won't have to move and—"

"You have to get out of here." He grabbed my hands. "I can't go, but you can."

Chris was an only child to a mother who had been too obese to leave her bed. In the past year, she'd made him proud by losing a hundred fifty pounds. Not enough to be comfortable, but enough to move around the trailer.

"Then come," I said. "I move, then you move and we meet far away somewhere."

He squeezed my hands. "Look at you. You can be anything you want. Go be it. That's all I have to say."

He looked over my shoulder, then back at my face. I knew him enough from our summer together to know I needed to wait to hear whatever he said next.

"I'll be here when you get back," he continued.

I almost lost my mind in his eyes. Almost agreed with him. I could do anything, but I didn't want to. I wasn't Harper, with her big dreams and bigger brain. I didn't have ambitions or a career in mind. I figured I'd inherit the factory and keep it going, or not. What I really wanted was a house full of people who depended on me.

"I'll think about it," I said because I wanted to make Chris happy for a moment.

"When do you have to be back?" he asked.

"Mom thinks I'm volleying with Marsha."

He brushed my knee with his fingertips. My skin felt as though it was melting underneath him and I became very aware of the hard trunk between my legs.

"Marsha's in the pool house with what's-his-face."

"Charles."

He leaned into me. "What do you think they're doing in there?"

They called Marsha a tramp, but I didn't think she was. Or maybe I thought being a tramp suited her. Or I thought it wasn't a big deal.

"Stuff."

"This, maybe?" He ran two fingers inside my thigh.

Sensation rushed behind them, to my knees, and ahead to the soft place between my legs. We'd kissed plenty in the back room of the pro shop and in the utility closet. He'd run his hands over my shirt, but he'd never touched me like that before.

"Maybe," I gasped.

I shouldn't let him run his hand up my other thigh. I should stop this right there. He was going way too fast. There were *steps* and he wasn't honoring them. But that made his touch even more explosive. My body didn't expect the speed of his advance, and it reacted by opening up all the way.

"Oh, my God." His eyes were wide and his lip was stretched

behind his top teeth. When he let it go, it went from white to deep pink. "Look at you. I can't believe how sexy you are."

My face tingled. Chris wasn't any more experienced than I was, but he was so open and honest about what he was doing and what he wanted that his words made me blush.

His index finger brushed the edge of my shorts. "Can I touch you?"

I throbbed when he asked. The ache inside me was almost painful in its need.

But was it too much? Would he think I was a slut? My legs were already open, by design. Wasn't that already an invitation? I could have swung both legs to one side, but I hadn't taken the modest posture.

In the pause after his question, he kissed me, pressing his thumbs into my inner thighs. His tongue in my mouth was such a sweet violation. I wanted more. All the more.

I picked up his hands and put them on my chest. Lips locked, he ran his thumbs over my hard nipples as I reached back, under my shirt, and unhooked my bra.

He broke the kiss. I came forward to put our mouths together again, but he leaned back. "Show me."

I would have preferred to kiss while he felt my breasts so it would feel as though I was in thoughtless throes of passion. It would feel less mindful. If we were putting thought into it, pausing and stopping, appreciating every act, then I had no excuse.

Chris gently pulled at the hem of my shirt. He didn't want mindless. He wanted to see every second. I knew my nipples were hard under my bra and he was looking at them as if he was savoring the sight. His relish shamed me and made my skin tingle at the same time.

In the choice between shame and the tingle, I made my choice.

I pulled my shirt up over my breasts. The bra lifted. He ran his hands along the underside before he pulled the bra up.

He sucked in a breath.

"These are beautiful." He bent my hard nipples before he gently squeezed them.

The feeling shot right between my legs as if connected by an electric wire. My back arched, and my consciousness hid behind a wall of pleasure.

The bough slipped from under me, and his hands tightened on my rib cage.

"Whoa, there," he said, keeping me from falling.

"I'm sorry."

"Don't be. Just remember where you are." Ever so tenderly, he pinched my nipples again. It hurt a little, but the pain was part of the pleasure. "Can you put your hands behind you? On the branch?"

He guided my arms behind me. My shirt fell back down, but once I was secure, leaning back against my locked elbows, he drew it up again. I was exposed to the sky.

"Next time, I'll do it your way." He pushed my chin up so I was looking through the branches at the clouds and ran his hand down my body. "I'll go up first so you can lean on the trunk."

"Yes, okay."

Both hands landed on my breasts. "I like it when you agree."

He kissed my sternum and twisted my nipples.

I groaned.

He twisted a little harder. "Do you like that?"

"Yes. Yes."

"You smell like roses." He sucked one nipple and hurt the other in a way that brought pleasure to the surface. I was filled with blood, my insides bigger than my outside, stretching my skin to thin translucence. "I should call you Catherine of the Roses."

"More," I gasped, the word falling out of my mouth like a piece of gum I'd forgotten about.

I didn't even know what I was saying. I was losing my mind as he worked me over. Blind, deaf, dumb. My whole body was wedged between his fingers.

My face was toward the sky, a curtain of dappled orange from the daylight on the other side of my closed eyes. A frame of white-hot shockwaves flickered in my vision, and something broke in me. I stopped thinking, breathing, feeling anything but him as the world pressed in on me and I pressed out into the world.

"Jesus!" he said when I finally gasped and opened my eyes.

"Oh, my G—"

"You *came*."

Sitting up straight, I put my hands over my face. I was ashamed. I'd done that, in front of him, from nothing. "I didn't think I would!"

When I took my hands away and saw him looking at me, I yanked my shirt down.

"It was awesome!"

Awesome? I wanted to die.

Lance yipped right before Harper's voice came past the fence.

"Catherine!"

Chris looked at his watch, but I didn't need to see it. Three p.m. had come and my bra wasn't hooked. I reached behind me and grappled with it.

I had to get down and Chris was in my way. He'd made me come right here, outside, in a tree. I was ashamed and nervous, and he was pulling my shirt down to cover me. He was beautiful, with his blue eyes and the wavy fall of hair over one side of his forehead. He was inappropriate. Unsuitable. Dangerous to my future, whatever that was.

"Hey," Harper called without shouting, as if she knew I was close by.

Chris climbed up a branch to get out of my way, indicating his handmade staircase, then putting his finger to his lips.

Lance stretched his chain to get to Harper, wagging his tail like windshield wipers in a storm. She crawled through the hole in the fence to pet him while looking all around.

"Cath?" she called.

"Coming!" I shouted, scuttling down.

"There you are!" She stood while Lance sniffed around her ankles. "Mom said to go to the car."

I slung my bag over my shoulder. "Okay, let's go."

"This is Lance, right? Is Chris around?" She pointed at the tree. "Were you climbing with him?"

"I'm sure he's working."

"Is that a ladder up the trunk?" She pinched her bottom lip until it creased.

I slapped her hand down. "Stop bending your lip like that. It's going to stay that way." I took the hand I'd slapped before she had a chance to bend her lip again, pulling her to the break in the fence. "And don't even think of climbing that tree. It's not safe." She went through first, and I followed. "I'm telling the grounds crew it's there before someone gets hurt."

My muscles didn't relax until we got to the car and I knew Harper hadn't seen Chris in the tree. If anyone knew the way he'd touched me and the way it made me feel, I'd die. Literally die.

CHAPTER 12

CATHERINE - PRESENT DAY

The squeaking upstairs was done, and the pipes rattled in the walls when the shower turned on. I read the final draft of my note for the hundredth time. Beginning to end.

Dear Chris,

Your letter came as a surprise. It's wonderful to hear from you after all these years. How they've flown by!

I am so sorry to hear about Lance. I think burying him at home is the right thing. I know Joan buried Galahad on Wild Horse Hill. You should get a space nearby.

Though it would be great to see you, I'll be unavailable while you're here. Please accept my condolences.

Sincerely,
Catherine

HARPER BOUNCED down the steps in a pair of little pink shorts. Taylor was at her heels. The way he followed her was so cute I smirked a little.

"There's a pot of soup on the stove if you're interested," I said.

"Thanks!" Harper went to the kitchen. She'd say she hated it because I'd used frozen peas and carrots, then she'd eat it anyway because she was a human vacuum.

On the way to the kitchen, still holding the half-crumpled letter, something overwhelming occurred to me.

Was Harper going to leave with this guy?

Leave the house?

Leave Barrington?

Leave *me*?

She did complain about the soup, and she ate it. She argued with Taylor about a laptop and bowls and I made all the right gestures and sounds, but I wasn't really there. I was sinking into a quicksand of things that hadn't occurred to me.

I had been glad to have Taylor around. Glad Harper was happy.

But it had never occurred to me that he'd take her away.

In the middle of the conversation, the letter took on a life of its own. I pulled an envelope out of the rack. It already had a stamp and a white label over my address. The post office hadn't canceled the stamp, so I'd kept it. The seal that had closed it wasn't sticky anymore. Nothing a little tape couldn't fix. It was a gem of an envelope.

Sending the note to Chris that way would make me look cheap, or worse, poor. But I put the crumpled paper in and snapped a piece of tape from the dispenser, pressing it down with my thumb as if getting every corner flat made the decision more final.

You're really doing it?

I'm really doing it.

"Harper," I said before she left with Taylor. They were picking something up at the store before church. "Can you mail this?"

She snapped it from me as if it were just another bill before leaving me alone in the house.

For the moment.

For the morning.

Soon to be forever.

CHAPTER 13

CATHERINE - SIXTEENTH SUMMER

Playground tonight. 10:30pm.

I left him the note inside my racquet case when I took it for restringing. It had been a full week since he touched me in the tree, a week since we'd spoken or since I looked him in the eye.

I'd been avoiding him. He'd said *hi* a few times and made sure we crossed paths. Once, he stood by the opening in the fence and gestured for me to pass through with him, but I turned and walked the other way.

I'd given him more than I intended up in the tree, and I couldn't bear it. I couldn't look anyone in the eye. They'd see right into my heart and call me a tramp like they called Marsha. Mom would stop being proud of me, and Dad would be ashamed. Harper would still love me, but what kind of example was I setting?

My shame outweighed my desire for him for five days. By the end of the week, shame was feather-light and desire broke the scales. I handed my racquet through the pro shop window and walked away, holding my breath until my parents went to bed and the house was quiet. I peeled off my nightgown to the clothes underneath and tiptoed out the side door.

My bike leaned up against the house. In the dark, I rode it down the service road to the place where the trees opened to the train tracks, then I left it against a tree.

I never realized crickets were so loud until I had to wonder if they were hiding the sound of my footfalls as I kicked up leaves and needles. I'd entered the deep brush, with the witness of owls and insects. A night creature with little nails scratched and crawled over my feet and made me jump. I hit a spider web and clawed through it as if I were fighting an invisible demon.

I didn't wonder so much if the animals could see me. I wasn't that paranoid. But whenever they moved or whenever a cricket jumped, I worried that a person could detect that someone was near and they could find me. Or they could ask me why I was even on this side of town.

I crossed the train tracks, looking both ways as if the freight ran on a thoroughfare. It was a few steps to the rows of mobile homes that defined that side of Barrington.

The playground was in a little clearing just west of the center of the trailers. My fingertips were cold, but the rest of my body thrummed and pulsed so hard that I made my own heat. I told myself I didn't know what to expect from this meeting, but if I didn't know what to expect, I knew what to hope, and they were pretty much the same thing.

"Catherine!" Chris wasn't loud, but the excitement in his voice made him sound as if he were shouting.

"Chris?" I spun around, looking for him in the darkness.

And on a three-quarter turn, he crashed into me, all lips and hands, digging his fingertips into the muscles of my back as he pulled me close. I tasted the minty toothpaste in his mouth and thought *he brushed his teeth for me.* He kissed me as if he would never kiss me again. He kissed me as if this was the last kiss he would ever have in his life. As if he wanted to eat me alive. I'd given over my freedom and my choice to this thing with him, to this moment, to this stupid set of choices that would ruin me forever. As surely as the sun would rise, I was the designer of my own destruction.

I wanted to be destroyed by that kiss.

When Chris took my hand, I imagined I could feel the blood pulsing through the veins, the cells in his skin. I imagined that when my nerve endings vibrated at his touch, they connected to his somehow.

Everything felt new. I was discovering that my body had routes between one place and another that I never knew existed. I never knew that when a man touched my hand or kissed my nipples, I could feel it between my legs.

There was a click behind the tree line, and he stopped kissing me with a jerk. We froze long enough for him to smile.

"I don't want you to do this anymore," he said. "It's not safe."

"It's fine."

"I'll come to you. Please. I've been worried since the sun went down."

Behind me, a twig snapped and I jumped. "I think I just proved your point."

"Just a squirrel. Come this way."

He led me to the play structure, and I giggled as I walked up the plastic ladder. I was so big I barely even needed to hit every step. I didn't really need him to hold out his hand and help me to the top of the slide. But I took it, because his touch was the spinning center of my curiosity.

The vantage point wasn't that much better than the ground, but I felt somehow encouraged to look out over the rows of trailers. Most of them had lights on, blue rectangles from flashing TV shows, the shouts, laughs, cries of kids getting ready for bed.

His body pressed me from behind, his hands drifted up and

down me. His lips brushed against the back of my neck. My eyes fluttered closed, and I sighed.

When he cupped my breasts over my shirt, I should have been ashamed. I should have run away. But I felt so safe with him. Even when he pressed his pelvis forward and I felt his erection on my bottom. I pushed my hips back against him and he breathed into my neck.

"Catherine, I want to make you come again."

Even in the tight lasso of his arms, I managed to turn around to face him. "It's your turn."

He tilted his head down a little and took my mouth in a kiss that was so much a question, not so much a permission as a demand. And I acquiesced, yielded to him completely. Our knees bent, and he ended up on the small floor, surrounded by gates, under an apparatus where a kid could change the times of day to match the sun and the moon. We barely fit on that little rectangle, but we were so twined up in each other that we didn't make any kind of reasonable or measurable shape.

"I want you," he said. "I want you so bad. I don't know what to do with myself all day. Whenever I feel rose petals, I think of your skin. I smell them, and I think of you. I stick my hands in the soil and think of getting my fingers inside you."

His words made me nervous. I'd never used words like that, especially with a boy. They seemed dangerous. He must have felt me freeze a little because he took my hand and put it between his legs. My God, he was so hard. I ran my nails along the length of him, through the fabric of his pants. I didn't know what I was doing, but I must have been doing something right because he let loose a breathy "ah."

He undid his jeans button, then the zipper, and guided my hand to the skin of him. I couldn't believe what I was doing and what it was doing to me. I felt how wet I was. The sensation at my core was going to take over and he wasn't even touching me.

I'm going to do this. I'm going to do what makes him happy.

I wrapped my hand around his shaft, feeling how the thin skin moved against the rigid core. "It's wet. Did you come already?"

"No, that's just a little bit that comes out at first."

With my thumb, I rubbed the liquid around the tip, and he kissed me so hard that my head was pushed up against the plastic floor.

"Move your hand a little bit." He wrapped his hand around mine and moved up and down. "Like that. Yes."

"Like this? This feels good?"

"Yes. Like that. You turn me on so much. I'm not going to rush you. I want to get inside you so bad."

I wanted him inside me. I wanted him to break through, tear me to shreds, open me, but I wasn't ready. I wanted to feel him in my hand before I felt him in my body.

His hips jerked rhythmically until I didn't have to move my hand so much. Still kissing me, he jerked back and forth, then he rolled onto his back with me on top of him and pulled up his shirt. We did everything with our lips still connected, as if moving away would break the moment.

He came onto his stomach. I was shocked how much there was, spurting all over him with white arcs in the moonlight.

"Thank you," he said into my mouth.

I kneeled next to him, the skin of my knees pressed into cold plastic. His bare torso was pooled with semen.

"What are we going to do?"

He dug a tissue out of his pocket and wiped it away. "We're taking care of you."

"What do you mean?"

Lazily, his hand drifted to my knee, then up my thigh and under my shorts. He pushed a little. "Spread your knees apart."

He didn't wait for me to do it. He slid his fingers under my clothes and touched me where I was wet.

"Oh." I couldn't do more than squeak.

His hand wrestled with the shorts and the underwear until he could angle a finger inside me. I exhaled sharply. I'd put my fingers inside before, but when he did it, I couldn't even think.

"I heard this isn't what works," he whispered. "Have you heard about the clitoris?"

"What?" Of course I had, but I didn't want an anatomy lesson.

"It's here, I think." He drew his finger out and up, finding the swollen nub.

"Oh, my God."

"Wow," he said in wonderment, running the back of his finger against it as much as he could in the tight space. "Is that it?"

"Uh-huh."

"Does it feel good?"

I fell back on my hands, knees off the floor, with his hand still up my shorts.

He rubbed too hard. Too fast. He was as clumsy and earnest as you'd expect from a teenager.

"I wish I could kiss it," he said.

And that was it. The thought of his lips sent shockwaves down my spine. I came into his hand.

When he pulled his hand out, he wiped his fingers with the tissue. We lay beside each other and watched the moon cross half the sky before we went home.

CHAPTER 14

CATHERINE - PRESENT

$\mathcal{H}$arper confirmed she'd sent the letter. I felt a kind of relief that I didn't have to see Chris. My excuse was in the world, on the way, out of my hands.

What I did with my life now was up to me. Harper had been able to take care of herself for years. I'd drained myself of almost every asset except the house itself for the sake of the people of Barrington. I had nothing left to give them, and the town itself had nothing left for me.

I'd been waiting for Chris and I hadn't even realized it.

But now that I'd made a decision not to see him, he was everywhere.

The rosebushes that had grown wild, the creaky floorboards, the knowledge that there were still flying monkeys scratched into the back of my great-grandfather's headstone.

The space behind the beige rotary wall phone led to a pantry, and the counter nearby was stuffed with pamphlets, flyers, phone books, recipes, and any other piece of paper we didn't know what to do with.

Since I was a teenager, numbers had been scrawled on the

wall around the phone. Mother wouldn't have liked it, but she did it first. And Dad, for his part, never saw any reason to update a phone that worked perfectly well.

In the ridge of molding was a number etched in quick little ballpoint lines. The dark blue had faded and the years of grease and dirt obscured it, but if I put my temple to the wall, it was still readable.

Chris's number hadn't worked in years. Not since his mother left Barrington and the trailer they'd lived in fell to the elements. I went into the pantry and sat where I always had when I wanted a little privacy—on the root box that hadn't stored a root in a decade. The peeling shelving paper had the same blue flowers, and the light hung dark and bald, kissing the silver ball chain.

For the first time since I'd sent Harper off with the letter, I felt its weight.

What had I done? If I'd been waiting for him all those years without realizing it, why reject him when he came? Shouldn't I be celebrating my success? My patience? The victory of maturity over whim?

Shouldn't I be cleaning the house and getting ready for him instead of telling him not to come? What was I supposed to do now?

I'd only done a couple of impulsive things in my life, and they all had his name on them.

It was Monday. I didn't usually cry until bedtime, but sitting on that root box, I wanted to wail my heart out.

"Catherine Barrington," I growled, "enough is enough."

When I came out of the pantry, Harper was already in the kitchen, leaning into the refrigerator. She wore her yellow shirt and a ponytail.

"Morning."

"Harper, what would you say if I went away?"

"Like what kind of went away?" She leaned her whole head into the refrigerator. "To prison or a trip?"

"A trip."

"I'd say 'have fun.'" She came out with yogurt, peanut butter, and jelly. "Where are you going?"

Where was I going? Anywhere.

"Paris." I said it as if it was the closest guess in a timed game show.

"Fancy. Nearest passport office is in Springfield. Do you need me to come?"

I didn't have a passport. If I wanted one, I would have to wait weeks to get it. I wanted to leave *now*. Tomorrow. Sooner. I wanted to go and get a new life before I lost my nerve.

"I don't know. Maybe."

"Taylor's staying here," Harper said. "I hope that's all right. He's harmless. And I only have a half shift."

"It's fine."

"I need extra cash for your birthday party." She put the containers in a plastic bag and snapped the loaf of bread off the counter without slowing down.

"What birthday party?"

"Thursday dinner barbecue." She kissed my cheek and headed for the door.

"Harper!"

The door slammed behind her. I'd forgotten about my birthday, but she hadn't. She loved me. She'd come back from college to help with Dad and never went back. She'd sworn she stayed because she wanted to, not to keep me company.

She'd lied, and I'd chosen to believe it. She and I were in this prison together. We were both going to be free.

I had to stay through the week. I guessed it was just as well. I could get a passport and take my time preparing to abandon Barrington.

Upstairs, I heard a crash that rattled the walls. Then another. I ran up, pausing in the middle of the staircase. In bare feet and a robe, I was in no condition for a man to see me. Even my sister's man.

I heard another crash. It was coming from my old room. The one after the first and before the place I slept now. The master suite Daddy gave me when he thought it would cheer me up.

The walls pounded again, vibrating top down as if they shook from fear. Taylor had asked me for tools a few days before to spackle over a mushroom growing from the bathroom ceiling. He hadn't asked for a sledgehammer.

I took the steps two at a time in my bare feet, running down the hall in leaping bounds as another crash came from the master suite. My suite. My space. The room that had been mine after Chris left, and the room I'd abandoned after a leak soaked the walls through and a mushroom grew on the bathroom ceiling.

A cloud of dust hung like a ghost outside the door. The window at the end of the hall caught each fleck of dust in morning light as they twisted and flew when I leapt inside it.

I froze at the threshold.

Taylor was in his late twenties. He was polite to Harper. He cleaned up after himself and spoke in complete sentences. Sweaty, stripped down to his undershirt, his skin was marbled with dirt and grime already. She'd said he was visiting from California, but she hadn't said he was a demolitions contractor or that he'd be plying his trade while she was at the distro center.

The bed was covered in a blue tarp, and the ceiling—which was a piece of tin painted over in pink roses—was dusty but intact. Thank God.

"Oh, my Lord!" I said when he noticed me there.

"Good morning." He had a beautiful smile for a guy I wanted to scream at.

"What… what are you doing?"

"Don't come in!"

"But—"

"There are nails."

The room seemed darker, no doubt because the plaster walls weren't reflecting the light from the French doors to the balcony. They were just exposed hundred-year-old wood. Yellow Xs had been marked on some of the beams where the wood had been damaged by mold.

"You won't have the mushroom again."

It took me a second to catch up to what he meant. The roof over the back of the house had leaked into the bathroom five years before, and since then, a long-stemmed mushroom had grown from the ceiling. We'd repaired the roof and plastered over the fungus every year, but every year it grew back stronger.

And it was gone. I was rendered speechless by his kindness.

"The mold isn't safe to breathe," he continued.

Safe. Funny word. My parents had put me in this room to keep me safe. And Daddy had Reggie paint the ceiling to soothe me while I was safe and miserable.

"And that?" Taylor pointed at the roses. "I looked behind it. It's clean."

Clean.

Another funny word. After my parents caught me with Chris, I found out what they each were obsessed with. For my mother, the issue had been cleanliness, and my lack of it. For my father, it was safety.

After all the crying. All the fighting. After I showered the blood off my leg and the sticky gunk off my belly, I could never be right again for my mother. But Daddy had done all he could to make it right, even if he did everything wrong.

When Chris left, this hadn't been my room. There hadn't been a rose-painted ceiling. Above me, two golden wings peeked out from a flare of petals, hidden cleverly by Barrington's only artist.

I'd been a different person, and this room was part of a different era.

But not really.

Who was Chris? Who was I? All those years... should I sweep them away? Pretend they didn't happen? Take the tin down, roll it up, and toss it aside? Pack up and run away so I could be sixteen again as if the flying monkeys hidden in the flowers had never existed?

I'd sworn to leave a minute ago, and now all I wanted to do was stay in my house with my people, taking care of a town I loved.

"I want to say something," I said to Taylor.

"Yes?"

"I own a gun."

"Okay?"

"I know how to use it."

He must have thought I was talking about Harper, because he went from swaggering to sincere. As if I'd threaten him over her. Anyone who knew Harper knew she could take care of herself.

"Cath—"

"Don't let anything happen to the painting."

He nodded slowly, as if he didn't understand why it mattered. "Yes, ma'am."

"And thank you," I said. "It'll be nice to sleep in here again."

I ran down the hall and threw myself onto my bed.

I wanted Chris to come to me, and I'd told him not to.

I wanted to leave so badly.

And I wanted to stay.

The tug-of-war for my heart raged, and I decided I was not going to shed a tear for it.

CHAPTER 15

CATHERINE - SIXTEENTH SUMMER

*M*y father kept the factory open even when seventy-five percent of the workers were gone and the skeleton crew didn't have much to do. He'd cut their hours, their insurance, their benefits. They understood, taking their lumps like warriors. Twice a year, on Memorial Day and Labor Day, he threw a free barbecue for anyone who wanted to come. Mom hated it because it was all Barrington people. She always invited her Doverton friends, but they turned up their noses. She claimed migraines and bellyaches, but she was expected to be there, same as the rest of us.

Some of Harper's elementary school friends were going to Montgomery High with her. She was awkward and too smart for her own good, but she was genuine. They found her tolerable because she wasn't interested in gossip and romance. She wasn't competition.

At the Labor Day barbecue, she abandoned her friends to their flirtations so she could run around with the litter of bloodhound puppies nipping at her heels. Reggie kept a booth with paintings of lightning bolts and rollicking planets. Juanita and

Florencio had a booth with *pupusas*. There were more crafts and energy in that square than any other day of the year. The rock music was provided by a bunch of guys from the public high school. Bernard, who was a year older than me and worked at the lumber yard, sang in a gravelly voice that was strangely dazzling.

I wasn't as awkward as my sister, but I didn't find the girls in my grade tolerable. They ranged from rigid religious anger-bombs to Doverton kids who found me beneath them. Marsha and I spoke, but not much outside school.

I stood on the grass, surrounded by my neighbors, each of them too poor, too crass, too unseemly to associate with. Listening to Bernard sing and watching my sister roll on the ground with a bunch of puppies, I was trapped, and yet, somehow free.

Leaning on the bleachers, Chris cracked peanuts between his teeth and spit the shells. I hadn't seen him in days and it seemed like years. Every time I saw the kick of his hips and the way his lips stretched across his teeth when he smiled, it seemed like the first time.

I watched him.

He watched me.

School started the next day. We'd go back into our different worlds. Would we meet again? Would we see each other at all? We'd grappled with the question by avoiding it.

A waft of smoke from the grills came between us.

We were alone. Surrounded by people, we were alone.

He pitched his peanut bag in the trash and washed it back with a bottle of off-brand cola. When he finished, he sucked in his bottom lip to catch an errant drop.

He tossed the bottle up. It spun in the air, and with a tap of his knuckle on its way down, he sent it into the trash.

I stepped toward him, and he stepped back. Not away. He stepped back toward something, flicking his finger that I should follow.

Easiest decision I'd ever made. It was barely even a decision.

I glanced around for Mom and Dad. They were in the gazebo with Badger, the new mayor, and his staff. Harper and the kids played with the puppies while Johnny and his wife watched. Lance jaunted around the perimeter, peeing on poles whenever he could, nipping back any sibling who got too big for their britches, ever the alpha.

I tilted directions slightly toward the bathrooms, then once past the bleachers, I saw Chris peeking from an alley between the hardware store and the library. I picked up my skirt and ran toward him, cutting the corner so hard I lost my balance. Out of nowhere, his hand was on my arm, keeping me from falling over.

Finger to lips, he led me to a black iron door. He clinked through his keys and opened it, stepping out of the way so I could pass through. We were in an office.

He closed the door with a loud *clap*, leaving the window as the only light.

"Chris?"

I barely got out the S before his lips kissed his name away. He put his hands on my jaw, keeping it still so he could invade my mouth. It felt good to give it to him. My body lost all its strength, held up only by the electrical currents between us.

"Catherine," he said in a breath, keeping his lips an inch from my face as he spoke.

"Where are we?"

"Back of the hardware store. I open on Thursdays."

"What are we going to do? I'm scared."

"Of me?"

"Of not seeing you anymore."

"I'll find you."

I clutched his shirt as if I'd be swept away without him. "I don't fit in anywhere. Harper is so smart she tolerates me. The only time I feel right, like I'm part of something, like I belong, is when I'm with you."

"One more year. Then you can go to college and I'll come after. We'll be so far away, we'll forget our names. When people ask where we're from, we won't even know."

"I don't know if we'll make it a year. I feel like they see us. Even now."

I must have been shaking, because he put his arms around me so tightly it hurt. I loved the pain of his attention. It was the pain of safety, of care, of being broken just enough for release.

"Harder," I said into his shoulder.

He squeezed me so tightly I could just barely breathe, and the tension rolled off me like water.

He let his arms go slack enough to look me in the face. "We'll make it. Then I'll follow you anywhere. I'll be your puppy dog."

"Oh, Chris, don't be silly."

"Don't deny me. I'm yours." He said the last word with a gusto I'd never associated with myself. As if life was something to grab with both hands and free like a bird that could carry us into the sky.

Together, we were freedom.

The bird launched from my chest and flew to my lips when we kissed again. Not a kiss of relief this time, but a kiss of passion. Ours was a kiss that began a string of thoughtless acts.

His hands slid down my body, grazing my breasts, landing at my waist. I felt the hardness under his jeans. I should have been scared, or freaked out, or ashamed, but I wasn't. I was free.

He broke the kiss and stroked my bottom lip with his thumb. "Should we go back?"

"No." I took his wrist and put his hand on the triangle below my belly.

He gasped and his lashes fluttered. Seeing that he liked it sent my body to the edge of common sense. This was crazy and I didn't care. Being the good girl hurt, and this felt good.

"My parents have to stay at the barbecue," I said. "That's their job."

He hesitated. Swallowed hard. Pinched a bit of my skirt fabric.

I nodded.

He pulled my skirt up until my cotton underwear was exposed. I ran my hand over his jeans, feeling his erection. He seemed harder and bigger than humanly possible.

When he kissed me again, I backed into the desk, leaning on it. Chris twisted his finger around my underpants leg. His touch was pure magic, and in the milliseconds before his finger hit home, it gathered enough electricity between my legs to power the entire factory.

I didn't realize how wet I was until he touched me.

"Oh, shit." His face contorted.

I could barely breathe. Standing up straight seemed impossible, so I let the desk bear my weight.

"Rin," he said, looking down between my legs.

My skirt was around my waist and my underwear was printed with roses. Old lady roses. My underpants looked like a dinner plate and his finger was stuck under them, ready to unleash otherworldly pleasure.

"Please, don't stop."

"I've never done this before."

"Me neither." I lifted his shirt just enough to see the line of light brown hair that disappeared under his waistband.

"I don't know how to make it good. And I don't have a condom."

"My period finished yesterday." I unbuttoned his jeans. "And it's going to be good. I know it."

Was I convincing him? Did that make me a whore?

As if the sound of my mother's voice in my head was audible to him, he took his hand out of my underwear. "I love you, Rin."

I melted and relaxed. You weren't a whore if it was love. Rushing things, maybe. But not a whore. Everyone knew that.

"I love you too."

With that, I unzipped his jeans. He kissed me, wrestling my underwear off while I got my hands on the stretched skin of his shaft.

Was I even real anymore?

Was I made of skin and bone or was it all just thick liquids vibrating in his direction?

Shifting my bottom back onto the desk, he wedged himself between my legs and slid his length along me. It felt so good— better than when I did it myself. Better than anything I'd ever felt in my life. I understood why adults wanted to keep us away from this. I'd beg and steal for it. I'd break walls and set the town on fire for what he made me feel. I was weak from it, and powerful inside it.

He ran it along the hard nub at the top again and again. I came, and when he kept on rubbing, I came harder, pressing my lips together to keep from screaming.

I didn't know if I'd broken some rule of sex etiquette by having an orgasm, but when he smiled at me, I knew it was all right by him.

"You're beautiful," he said. "I'm never going to forget what you look like right now."

He'd seen me. Watched it. Shame was like a snake in the basement, ready to slink up the steps and under the door. I felt it coming. I could hold it at bay, but I knew it was there. The only way to block it was with more sex. More vibrations. More Chris.

I still wanted him. The orgasm hadn't made me want it less.

His bare head slid up to my opening as if drawn by the force of my desire. We were a gasping, sore-lipped, sweaty mess. I pushed my hips against him. Now. I wanted him to enter me immediately.

"Here goes," he whispered.

"Here goes."

He forced himself inside me. I bit back the pain. It wasn't too bad, but he stopped.

"Are you—"

"I'm fine. Go."

He didn't go. He looked confused, unsure.

"Please," I said. "If you love me, then make love to me."

Love. Always the great convincer.

He pushed all the way down to his base, stretching me as I'd never been stretched before. Slowly sliding his body into mine. Then out. Slowly. He closed his eyes and grunted deep in his chest.

I ran my fingers through his hair, pulling him down to me. He kissed my cheek and slid inside again, watching my expression. He hurt me less than last time. Maybe he could tell, because the next thrust was harder. Really hard. It pushed the air out of my lungs.

Did people talk during sex? I didn't know how.

I managed to get out a single word. "More."

As if I'd opened a gate and let a bull charge through, he pulled out and slammed into me again. And again. Harder and faster. Then slow and deep. Pleasure welled up inside me. Hard. Fast. Slow. I never knew what was coming next and it made me throb all over. His lips on my cheek, one of his hands leveraging the desktop as the other grabbed my ass, he grunted hard and pulled out.

"Wha—?" I didn't finish.

With his fist moving fast along his shaft and my naked legs spread wide in front of him, he closed his eyes and spurted on my belly.

I was appreciating the warmth and the look on his face. I was thinking about how this dishonorable thing of having my legs spread where he could see everything was actually pleasurable and freeing.

But as he was coming on me, a dog yipped outside. Lance, for sure. Then someone rapped on the window above. A man's voice came through the glass.

"Catherine Barrington!"

I saw Chris first, looking out the window with his hand around himself, his face lit in stripes by the iron bars. Then I bent my head back.

The man at the window was Sheriff Brady, and the horrified woman next to him was my mother.

WE HADN'T THOUGHT about the blood. It wasn't much, but it seemed as if it was everywhere. We scrambled to get dressed as Sheriff Brady used his universal key to get in. Lance came in first and sniffed our ankles. My skirt had twisted, leaving a streak of blood on the fabric over my left thigh. Chris barely had his pants up when Brady threw him against the wall so hard his head bounced against it. Lance bit the cop's pant cuffs, growling like the puppy he was.

"Stop!" I shouted.

But my father, who I hadn't seen through the window, took me by the arm in a skin-twisting grip. My eyes adjusted to the light as he pushed me outside. I yanked away, but he held me tight as a bird in the hand.

"That boy's going to be sorry," my mother said from behind me. "He forced you, obviously."

"He didn't." I was sure she didn't hear me, so I looked back and said it again. "He didn't force me."

"Of course he did."

Dad loosened his grip. He wouldn't look at me.

"This is humiliating," Mom continued.

The grassy square was visible in the slit between buildings. My shirt stuck to me where Chris had unloaded, and I tried to cover the blood with my hand. My thighs slid against each other from dripping fluids. I wondered if Sheriff Brady was going to return the underwear I'd left behind or if the office manager of the hardware store would find them.

The sheriff's black-and-white car was parked up the street, its windows wide open.

"Don't hurt Chris," I said. "I'll be good. I'll never see him again."

"I know," grumbled my father, lighting a cigarette.

"We'll discuss *him* later," Mom interjected.

"Daddy?"

"Don't worry about it, Peanut."

"I'm not letting you go soft, Earl." We broke into the town square and my mother brightened, giving me a sidelong glance. "Smile, darling."

Dad shook hands with some of the guys and talked the way men talk when a bunch of them get together. I could still see the police car. No Brady. No Chris.

Mom waved at my sister. "My God, look at her. Harper, dear! Come along! It's time to go."

"Maaaaa, noooooo." Harper's shoulders dropped and her knees bent as if leaving was a grievous hardship.

One split-second look of sternness got her to wave good-bye to the puppies.

"What happened?" Harper poked the blood-soaked spot on my skirt.

Mom slapped her hand away. "Stop asking questions." She put her hand on my father's shoulder. "Time to go, honey."

"Just a flesh wound," I whispered to my sister. Was she looking at the way my shirt stuck to the now-cold slime on my belly?

Harper scrambled into the limo. Behind me, Dad dropped his cigarette and smothered it with his shoe. I stole another glance at the police car.

It was gone.

I was sure Chris was in it. I was sure he didn't have the money to get out of trouble. Whatever that trouble was, it was going to be decided by my parents. His mother could barely get out of bed to go to court. How would she defend him? He had no one. It wasn't fair. I loved him and it wasn't fair.

"Get in," Mom snapped over my shoulder.

I put my hand on the doorframe and straightened my arm, locking it at the elbow. "No."

"Catherine," Dad said softly. "Let's just get home and discuss this." He arched an eyebrow and indicated the back seat with a quick tilt of his chin.

"Promise Chris will be all right and I'll get in."

"That boy is not going to be all right," my mother said.

"Then I'm going to go find him."

"Get in this car!" Mom's face was red.

"We're going to run away together and you'll never see me again!"

"Catherine Daisy Barrington." My mother's arm was stone-stiff, extending toward the door.

"Peanut," my father said gently, expectantly, threateningly all at once.

"I'm old enough to marry him." I took a backward step toward the town square. "I'll do it. If anything happens to him, I swear I will."

They looked at each other, then at me, then each other again, speaking in the silent way married people do. I had an opening.

"Promise you'll call Sheriff Brady as soon as we get home."

"I will not—"

I took two steps closer to the square. "Promise!"

I was losing my nerve by the second. I didn't have the strength to do what I threatened to do. I had to keep Chris first in my mind. The consequences for him were worse than a bad reputation. They'd get him fired. Send him to jail. Kick him out of school. Drain whatever money he and his mother had.

"Don't hurt him." I shifted my gaze to my father.

"Can you just grab her, Earl?"

"For what?" He seemed baffled. "If she's not going to ruin her life today, she'll do it tomorrow."

Wait.

Was that a promise?

Could I get in the car before someone passed close enough to see my sticky, bloody clothes? I looked from Mom to Dad as they killed each other with their stare.

"I need satisfaction," Mom growled.

"Get it somewhere else," he said before he looked at me. "Princess, we have a deal. I won't hurt him."

"You won't get him fired from the club?"

"Oh, for the love of…" Mom threw her hands up. "Now I can't go to the club?"

"I won't go anymore," I said. "I don't like tennis anyway. I just won't see him. Ever. Never again. Just… no charges. No lawyers. Promise."

Dad answered before Mom could object. "That's a fair deal."

Mom covered her face with her hands. While she was blinded by her humiliation and frustration, I caught my father's eye.

"Thank you," I mouthed silently.

He pointed at the car.

I got in.

CHAPTER 16

CATHERINE - PRESENT

It was down to me. My decision. Stay? Go?

Chris's letter had woken me from a deep sleep, and my letter back had stunned me into a fugue. My decisions were my own from now on.

Stay or go?

Not for him. Not to wait, or to pretend to myself I wasn't waiting.

Just what did I need? What did the people I loved need?

Which master did I serve?

A half dozen little elves came to the house, armed with brooms and buckets. I knew them as Juanita, Mrs. Boden, Pat, Sally and Trudy Crenshaw, and Dina Marcus. I was shooed out of my kitchen and left to go around the outside of the house so I wouldn't step on wet floors. I wasn't allowed down the hall where the suite was because another half dozen elves were fixing it. Harper was holed up in her room on the third floor. Taylor dragged his dirty, dusty self up there with plates of sandwiches and came right down after dropping them off.

"Is she eating?" I asked.

"Shoo," he said, then kissed my cheek before trotting down the hall to the dusty suite.

The house was packed with people who loved me, but none of them knew what I was going through.

I still didn't know if I was staying or going.

Counting the days, I waited until I could be reasonably sure Chris had gotten the letter. Then I did nothing. He'd gotten it by Wednesday, for sure. Done is done. I had nothing else to say to him. That part of my life was over now. It ended not with a bang or a light, but with an exhale.

Wednesday, the evening before my birthday, I was in my old room, the one that faced the front of the house. Everything was quiet and dark. This was about the time I'd let the sadness creep in and I'd cry myself to sleep. I hadn't cried in a week, but I'd slept well.

I didn't know how to feel about anything.

On Thursday, voices from across the house and clopping foot-steps along the hall told me people had arrived to work on the suite. I knew how I felt about that at least. Whether I stayed or went, I was glad to see the room taken care of.

I crossed my bedroom naked after my shower. My closet was open because I'd been looking for things to wear to my party later. A full-length mirror hung inside the door and I caught a glimpse of myself.

Most of my friends from school were in town. At nearly thirty, their bodies had been through childbirth at an early age, recovered, and done it again. My body had barely been touched.

My hands slid along my curves. My breasts, belly, hips, round and tight with disuse. All this skin was meant to be touched. It was designed to feel, to receive, to sense and interpret. My breasts were meant for children and the touch of a lover. They remained high and tight from neglect. Hardening under my fingertips, they were ready, and I was too.

I sat on the bed in front of the mirror.

This was me.

I spread my legs.

Still me. The little pink split had a function. I slid my finger there and felt the wetness that reminded me that it was ready. It worked. It could do what it was built for.

Moving my fingers along the liquid folds of skin, I quietly brought myself to orgasm without thinking of Chris until it was over.

"I'm sorry," I whispered into the sheets.

I didn't apologize to the Chris of today or even five years before, but to the sixteen-year-old boy who'd loved me. I'd let him go. I hadn't chased him. Hadn't fought for him. Hadn't looked for him or asked his mother what happened to him. And now I was releasing him with regret. But I was releasing him.

I washed my hands and dressed.

When I opened the door, I gasped. Reggie was in the hall with his fist up as if he was about to knock.

"Oh, sorry!" he said. "I was just—"

"It's fine."

"I wanted to tell you something." The paint splatter on his overalls was multicolored from years of spills and hard work.

"Okay."

Behind Reggie, Taylor carried a can of paint in each hand.

"Don't look," Taylor said to me before tapping Reggie in the behind with a can. "Come on, lazy ass. Let's get this done."

"I'm coming, Cali-boy." Reggie turned back to me. "Private."

I didn't have a place for him to sit in my room, so we went to the front porch. I sat on the swing, and he leaned on the railing. The hardware store delivery truck was just pulling away.

"What's all that?" I pointed at a stack of four moldy boxes in the corner of the porch.

"Found 'em in the crawlspace over the ceiling. You should check inside. See if there's anything you want."

I couldn't imagine anything of real or personal value in those collapsed, water-damaged, mold-covered boxes. They probably had mushrooms growing in them. I wrinkled my nose and sat back on the porch swing.

Reggie looked at the floorboards, rocking a little as if he was telling himself to get on with it. I folded my hands in my lap and waited.

"You know, I been looking at that ceiling for two days now. I musta been outta my mind."

"Why?"

"Painting roses on a tin ceiling? God, Catherine, nobody does that. You can paint it a flat color... but flowers? I bet that's the only tin ceiling mural in the United States."

"You should be famous."

"Hell, yeah. I've been telling myself that a long time now." He ran his fingers through his hair. "You know I... ah... well I remember when your father asked for it. You were sixteen and I was engaged to Carla the cheating bitch. But you, girl? You broke my heart. Like..." He squeezed his fingertips to his chest and exploded them like a starfish.

"It was a rough time."

After Chris left, my parents started the process of splitting up while living in the same house. Everyone knew it. There weren't many secrets in Barrington.

"You sure could peel the paint off with your crying." Reggie shook his head slowly with a smile. "Shit, I thought them flowers wouldn't survive with all your wailing."

I laughed to myself.

Seeing I wasn't hurt, he continued. "I thought to ask you to a job site, you know, save us some work with the scrapers." He laughed with me. "Thought we could even go international with it."

"Oh, Reggie, do you remember when I asked you to hide flying monkeys in it?"

"I thought you'd gone crazy. But your dad said to just do it."

"I loved them. I put the bed right under them so I could see them when I went to sleep."

"I'm glad. I'm really glad you got comfort from it. And I'm sorry you had to wait so long to get that room fixed up."

"I'm sorry I never asked."

"Thing is..." He looked away, then at me. "It was always something. You were real young. Then I got married." He ran through the list more quickly. "Then the factory closed and I was out of work. Then I got divorced. Then your father died. Then your mother left and you spent the next seven years taking care of everyone in this place like it's your job. It's the most beautiful thing I've ever seen. I never got to tell you how I felt about you, and now Chris fucking Carmichael is coming back and I got a sliver of a window to tell you."

"You don't have to," I said. Chris wasn't coming, which put the burden on me to refuse Reggie. He was a good man, but I couldn't lead him on. I didn't feel for him what I'd felt for Chris, and I wanted nothing less.

"I want to. I have to."

"Reggie, don't."

"I love you. I've always loved you and I don't care if you know it. I don't care if Chris comes back on a white horse and sweeps you off your feet or whatever. I'll be okay with that. But if he doesn't, I want you to know that you and me? We can talk if you want." He took a deep breath as if he'd needed to get that off his chest.

He and I didn't have anything to talk about. At least, not what he wanted to talk about. If he wanted to talk about how to get over waiting for someone who was never coming, maybe we'd have something to say to each other.

"Okay," I said, not ready to tell him there would be no Chris. No knight riding in on a white stallion. No fairy tale ending. That was my problem. Not his.

"Okay." He snapped his fingers as punctuation. "Now that we got that out of the way, I better go make sure they don't try to paint over my ceiling."

"Thank you. For everything."

"I ain't even done yet." He tapped the doorjamb twice and went inside.

CHAPTER 17

CATHERINE - SIXTEENTH SUMMER

I showered and then stayed in my room. I crouched on the floor with my knees to my chin and cried as they fought downstairs. Their voices came up the walls and into my room. I couldn't hear most of it. Phrases and words. The sun set and the room went dark. My throat was dry and my eyes throbbed.

Harper knocked and peeked around the door, letting in a shaft of light. "Hi." She stepped all the way in. "I came to say good night."

"Good night."

"What are they fighting about?"

"Me."

She sat on the bed, folding her nightgown between her knees. "Did you do something?"

"Yeah."

"What?"

"I can't say."

"Okay." She extended the last bit of the word as a launching pad into a run-on sentence. "Because I know you know everything, but it really sounds like they're mad at each other when she's calling him things I can't repeat and he's like—'well, after what you did, you have no business blah blah' and she's like 'your forgiveness is worse than revenge,' so there's that."

I put my head against the wall. "I don't know what they're mad about anymore."

"Yeah. Well. Do you want me to stay in here with you? Keep you company?"

I did. I wanted my sister's warm body kicking me all night. It would be worth it to prove I wasn't too filthy to love. But Mom didn't like when we curled up together, and it wasn't a good night to displease her.

"I think you'd better not. I'll be okay."

She kissed my cheek. "I love you."

"I love you too. Close the door on the way out, okay?"

She left me in the dark. Exactly where I wanted to be. On the floor, in the dark. When I got tired, I laid my cheek on my knees. I could have gotten into bed, but I didn't feel worthy of a comfortable pillow and clean sheets.

A cracking noise woke me.

I was on the floor under the window. The arguing downstairs was gone, replaced by crickets and the gurgling of the river. My neck hurt.

Pock. The sound came again.

It was the wall outside. I got up to my knees and looked out.

Pock.

A swoosh of yellow curved across my vision. I followed it down to the boy who caught it.

"Chris!" I didn't shout. I barely whispered, but his name echoed through me. I opened the window.

"You're there!" he said.

92

"What are you doing here?"

"I need to talk to you."

I couldn't see him well. I couldn't tell if he'd been roughed up or if he was upset. "Are you all right?"

Before he answered, I heard a noise in the hall. The squeak of a floorboard. Then another. I put the window down and jumped into bed, forcing myself to breathe slowly even though my heart was pounding and my lungs demanded more air, faster.

Someone came into the room and closed the door. The moonlight behind my eyes went dark as whomever it was blocked the window. Were they facing me? Or Chris?

I opened one eye.

Daddy stood over me.

"You're awake," he said, sitting on the edge of the bed. The mattress tilted from his weight. "How are you doing?"

"I'm okay." I rolled onto my back and pushed myself up, making an effort to not look at the window. "I'm really sorry about it. Today."

"Are you?" He smelled freshly showered. His hair was slicked back and his fingernails hadn't seen a day's work.

"I wasn't trying to embarrass you guys."

He sighed. "Look. Catherine. I want to ask you something, and I want you to be completely honest with me."

"Okay."

"Did you consent?"

I swallowed. If I said yes, I was a slut. If I said no, a rapist was waiting under my window. "I did."

He didn't seem shocked or scandalized. Didn't even seem bothered. "Did he hurt you in any way?"

His manner comforted me. Daddy was the kind of guy people liked just because they did, and I was no different than they were. I wanted to be honest. I wanted to please him. Mostly, I wanted to give him the answer that would get him to leave before Chris got impatient and threw things at the window again.

"I think just the normal hurt for the first time."

"Are you sure?"

"Pretty sure. It's not like I have a lot of experience. Or him either."

"It was his first time?"

"Yes."

Daddy tapped his fingertips together, elbows on his knees, looking between his feet. "I promised you I wouldn't hurt him."

I swallowed a lump of fear, going rigid with it rather than leap in front of the window to shield Chris. "You did."

"I'm glad I don't have to break that promise."

The fear went away and was replaced by curiosity.

Daddy turned on the bed until he faced me all the way. "I would have broken it if he'd forced you. I would have poisoned every part of his life. But how can I? You're old enough. You're the same age. You both agreed. The only misery here is the misery we're causing you."

I must have looked as if I saw Santa coming down the chimney, because that was how I felt. If he was admitting we hadn't done anything wrong, then he had to let Chris be my boyfriend.

"And," he continued, putting his hand on my arm as if to steady himself, "and we're going to continue to make you miserable, but in a different way."

"What kind of way?"

"The way parents do. We know what's best for you."

My heart sank. That last sentence was never spoken before good news.

"Your mother has a point. That boy is not right for you. He'll bring you nothing but heartache."

"Dad—"

"Wait. Listen to me. I want things to go smoothly for you in life. We've made sure you have an easy time of it. There are a thousand ways you can screw it up and we're here to point them out. Keep you from doing them. This is one of those ways. I've seen enough of the world to know that it's hard when you don't stick to your own kind."

"He is our kind."

He shook his head. "No, I'm sorry to say he's not."

"Daddy, please."

"Here's what your mother and I agreed to. We've spoken to his mother, and she's on board as well. You stay away from each other and everything's going to be all right. But if you don't, you'll spend your senior year at St. Thomas School."

"Where is that?"

"In Austin."

"What? That's forever away!"

"And I can't speak for whether or not he'll be able to continue to work at the club if you two are caught together again."

"You'll get him fired?"

"I'm sure it won't come to that." He stood. "I know you hate this. If you knew what your mother wanted to do, you'd be thanking me. Maybe someday you will."

I didn't answer. Didn't even look at him. I just stared at the triangles my bent knees made under the covers. When I was little and Daddy had his knees bent like that, I'd slide down them. I couldn't believe there had ever been a moment in my life when I wasn't this mad at him.

He stood there a long time. "Your mother and I are going to switch the rooms around."

I looked up at him, then at the window. Did he know Chris was downstairs? Had I already ruined everything? I needed to see him. Make sure he was all right.

"Since I work late," he continued, "we're taking separate rooms. Maybe you'd like the big suite? It has its own bathroom. I think at your age it's appropriate."

"Sure."

He leaned down and kissed my forehead. I crossed my arms so he didn't think I wasn't mad.

"You'll feel better about it in no time. And you can paint the suite any color you want."

"Thanks."

"I love you, Princess."

"I love you too, Daddy."

My arms were still crossed when he closed the door behind him. After the click, I leapt out of bed and opened the window.

Chris came out of the bushes.

I was about to call down to him. Tell him everything down the height of the house and the space across the front yard, but as he stepped forward, he was drowned in yellow light.

The porch lights. Someone had turned them on.

If he was seen there, it was all over.

He didn't need to be told. He jumped behind the bushes, and a second later, my father stepped out from under the porch roof, walking toward where Chris hid. I held my breath. I could see his hiding space clearly from the second floor, but had no idea what Daddy could see, or if he'd known all along that Chris was down there.

The porch light snapped off.

My father opened his car door and got in. The headlights bathed the driveway in light, getting smaller and smaller as he headed away from the house and turned onto Dandelion Road.

Chris didn't come out until the crickets and night birds filled the air with sound again. He was going to call to me and my mother could hear. My parents' room, the one I was about to paint any color I wanted, was on the other side of the house, but I couldn't risk getting caught.

I lifted the screen and leaned out. I wanted to say this once and I wanted to be heard. "Wait for me."

I closed the window before he could answer. I put on a robe and shoes with soft soles. I was sure they looked ridiculous with my nightgown, but I didn't want to get fully dressed.

If I had on pants and a shirt, I could leave with him right away. We could steal into the night. Never see Barrington again.

Pants. All I needed was a full set of clothing and I'd be ready. I'd be free.

Without really deciding it, I pulled my nightgown over my head and kicked off the shoes. Jeans. Bra. Clean dark blue T-shirt that would disappear in the dark of night. Socks. Sneakers for running far away.

I stopped before I closed the door.

There was something else.

I stood on a chair to get to the top shelf of the closet to retrieve a shoebox. Inside were photos of Harper and me. A spelling bee medal. An old pearl pin from Grandma. And an envelope. Flipping open the flap, I checked the contents. Seven hundreds, each from Grandpa on my dad's side. One for each birthday I had before he died. Two twenties earned for the two times I squeaked by with all As. A few singles from the few times I thought I'd put away some money.

Seven hundred forty-nine dollars got stuffed into my back pocket.

I knew where the creaky floorboards were. I tiptoed around them. I had to go past my parents' suite to get to the stairs, but they usually slept with the door closed. I jumped when I heard a squeak and a breath from the spare room. The door was open halfway.

Someone was in there, and it wasn't Harper.

Careful.

So careful.

I got past without a complaint from a single floorboard. Now, the suite would appear and I'd have to just be quiet...

But the door was open and the room was empty.

A second parent was somewhere in the house and I was wearing jeans and sneakers as if I was ready to run away. If I'd stayed in my robe, I could have said I was going downstairs to get a glass of water or something.

Okay, well. This was going to be what it was.

I went downstairs, skipping the loose boards. I left through the side door and went to the front, where Chris was. He must have known I was coming that way, because he met me halfway and kissed me before I could get a word in.

"I've been going crazy." He stopped long enough to speak, but not long enough to listen. He was all hunger.

I had to push him away. I put my finger to my lips and pointed up at the guest room window, then at the backyard. We tiptoed to the back like thieves. He led me past the white fence, into the cemetery. Past Hubert and Edith Barrington. Past Timothy Barrington, who built the house in his old age, His young wife, Alice, and his dead child, Frieda. We crouched behind Richard, who had been buried by the river before the house was even built.

Between two rosebushes where it was dark as a cave, Chris and I kneeled with our arms around each other.

"Do you swear you're all right?" I asked. He looked fine. I touched his face and didn't feel a bruise or bump.

"Nothing I can't handle. How are you? Your eyes are swollen."

"It's horrible. Everything's just horrible. I can't take another minute."

He held my jaw on both sides and looked into my face. "You can. You're strong."

I'd never thought of myself as strong. I only did what was easiest. Doing what I was told was easier than thinking about what I wanted. Chris was the only rule I'd ever broken because once he flirted with me at the club, he was too hard to stay away from. Once he kissed me, I didn't have the strength to refuse him.

"Only because of you," I said.

"I don't want to get you in trouble. I'm sorry I came."

"I'm glad you did."

"I couldn't wait."

"I'm ready. I don't need anything. We can just leave. Right now."

He pulled away, keeping his hands on my shoulders. I could barely see the whites of his eyes in the moonlight, but his voice was clear and urgent. "No, Rin. This is never going to be right between us."

"What?"

Was he breaking up with me? Had he lied? Had I given a liar my body?

"If we run away, I'm ruining your life. We're going to be two poor kids with nothing. Living on the street. Something has to change and I have to be the one to change it."

"What are you going to change? My family isn't changing. Barrington isn't changing."

"But I can change."

"Change into what? A rich man? Here? Pruning rosebushes?" I was sorry I said it the moment the words left my mouth. They were all true, but certain truths were unspoken.

Chris didn't seem hurt. His expression confirmed that we understood the same truths. "Not here."

"Where? I don't understand. You just said we weren't leaving."

When he slid his palms off my face and folded my hands into his, I knew what he intended to do.

"You can't leave me here," I said.

"I have to. Your parents are right. I'm not worthy of you. I have nothing to offer you."

The bushes closed in on me. The sky got low, the house inched closer, the river hemmed me in.

"Yes, you do." A sob choked back the rest of the sentence. What about happiness? What about love? What about two people making something out of nothing? "What about Lance?"

"I'll take him with me."

"Me too. Take me too."

"You have to finish here. It doesn't matter if I drop out of school," he said, trying to be comforting, "but you—"

"I need to graduate?" I couldn't let him finish his lie. "For what? Why does it even matter? I'm not Harper. I'm coasting."

He squeezed my hands so hard it hurt. I cried for real, but not because of the pain. I wanted it to hurt. I wanted to be pressed so hard my bones broke and the agony leaked through the cracks.

"I'm coming back," he said. "I'll get something going and come back for you."

"When?"

"Soon. I swear it."

Soon?

Barrington was a prison. What was soon to its prisoners?

And if he wanted to go, why would I keep him here? Why wouldn't I let him save himself? Why wouldn't I want better for him?

In that, I found a little bit of strength. It came from the same place as the double-dog-dare I'd laid on my parents that afternoon. I wanted to be with him. I needed him to come back, but setting him free to become all the great things he wanted to be was a source of power.

"Chris Carmichael." The tears stopped as if I'd twisted the faucet. I pulled my hands out of his, and he looked up in surprise and a little fear. "I swear to you, right now, and I mean it, I am not going to be with anyone else. I am here the same as always. So if you go off and do whatever? Change? Get a job? Find someone else?"

"I won't."

"Shush. If you do, you'd better write me and set me free, because I'm waiting for you."

"Okay."

"Say you understand."

"I understand."

"Say you'll tell me right away if there's someone else."

"I'll... there's no—"

"Chris!" I said through my teeth. "Say it!"

"Catherine Barrington, I swear that if I lose my mind and find someone else, or maybe, like, if an army of winged wild monkeys hold—"

"Winged monkeys?" I laughed as I wiped my eyes.

"Or feral unicorns."

"How far away are you going?" I tried to laugh quietly and ended up crying. He held me tight and kissed my hair. I rested my head on his shoulder.

"If I'm insane, or trapped, or if I'm possessed by the devil, I might come across another woman who's entirely wrong for me. Before I commit to a lifetime of misery with her, I'll set you free."

"Okay."

"Okay."

What now? Was he going to walk away and leave me behind a gravestone?

I wouldn't let him. He wasn't going to turn his back on me.

I stood. He got to his feet and tried to touch me, but I pushed him away. I wanted to frustrate him. Let him feel what I was feeling before he went off to make himself into a man.

"I'm going in the house," I said. "Please stay here until you're sure I'm in bed. Wait as long as you can. Then just go."

"Can I kiss you good-bye?"

"Promise you'll take care of yourself."

"I promise."

He leaned in for a kiss, but I pushed him away. When I leaned back, I felt the stiff mass of money in my pocket. My hand shot back to make sure it didn't fall out.

"No," I said. "I don't want some last kiss you have to appreciate. You should have known the last one was going to be the last."

"You're punishing me?"

I slid the envelope out of my back pocket. "Here." I slapped his chest with it.

"What...?" He opened it and thrust it back at me. "I can't take this."

"How much do you have on you?"

"It doesn't matter. I'm not taking it."

"You are. If you fail, you don't come back. I'm invested in your success."

He wavered, then came back to his original answer. "No."

"It's been sitting in my closet."

"I said no!"

"It's my guarantee!" I hissed. "You'll come back to pay me if nothing else. Even though I don't need it, because I live in a mansion with a staff and everything, you'll get back here to pay back a stupid seven hundred and forty-nine dollar loan. So take it or I'm going to think you want to cut me out of this deal entirely."

I snapped the envelope out of his hand and stuck it down his shirt. He laughed.

"Fine. But this is a guarantee," he said. "I pay my debts. I'm coming back with the money and more."

"Okay."

"And when I do, I'm bringing you a rose for every dollar."

"Just don't take them out of this garden or Mom's going to freak out."

He smiled. "Okay, deal."

"Deal."

We had nothing left to say. I sucked my lips between my teeth to fill the vacuum where words should have been. I already felt a little more distant, a little more cut off, a little more alone.

"Stay here until I'm in my room," I said.

I stepped back but couldn't do it. Whatever strength I had wasn't enough to deny my own need to kiss him. I had all the strength I needed because of him, but none to stay away from him.

Clutching the back of his shirt, his fingers in my hair, the force of his body against mine, I thought if I could just enter him, crawl inside him, he could take me along. Maybe that dream could happen. Two people making it work despite all the odds.

When I told myself the truth—that no matter how much I wanted to be with him every second, the odds were bad for a reason—I pulled away.

"You're going to wait here, right?" I asked.

"Yes." His arms relaxed and fell away.

"I love you," I said, stepping back until I could see all of him.

"I love you too. Always."

Not another word. Not another kiss or breath. Not another sight.

He'd forever be in the back of my family cemetery with his hands reaching for me and his lips claiming an eternity he didn't own.

I ran to the house without looking back.

103

I DIDN'T SLEEP that night. I didn't hear him leave and I didn't check.

In the morning, the back of my great-grandfather's headstone had a crude picture of an animal with wings and message scratched into it.

Not even winged monkeys

Not even.

PART II

CHAPTER 18

CHRIS

Dear Chris,
Your letter came as a surprise. It's wonderful to hear from you after all these years. How they've flown by!

𝒥'd arranged for Lance to be buried on Friday morning. The body had been transferred. The plot purchased. A little stone tablet would say *Lancelot Carmichael, Brave Knight. Marked territory in Barrington and New York City, 2004-2017.*

Just because Catherine didn't want me wasn't enough reason to insult Lance's memory. And maybe I'd find a reason to knock on her door and see if she was home.

I flew into the landing strip outside town and took a cab into Doverton, where the club had a car for me. I didn't tell the driver who I was or why I was there, sure that I was as anonymous as I'd always been. My life in Barrington had been in the shadows, behind hedges, forgotten and never known by anyone but the girl in the tree. The girl on my lips. Catherine of the Roses.

As we passed Barrington, I saw the roofline of the factory her father had owned. Nothing new had popped up. No new businesses or signs. Exactly the same.

I could have asked the driver to make the turn onto the factory service road. I could have walked over the bridge to her house or pulled right up to her front door.

I am so sorry to hear about Lance. I think burying him at home is the right thing. I know Joan buried Galahad on Wild Horse Hill. You should get a space nearby.

THE LETTER WAS SO cold I could feel her effort to contain herself inside the page. I thought about why and knew it wasn't anything as simple as another man. If there was someone, she'd invite me to dinner with him and we'd reminisce about everything but the way she gave me her body. There was more to it, and it was obvious. I'd written to her until I stopped. Those letters might have meant something to her, and I'd stopped because I needed a response she might not have been able to give. I'd abandoned her. I had no right to her. She wasn't obligated to save me from a meaningless life I hated.

Though it would be great to see you, I'll be unavailable while you're here.

SHE WAS UNEQUIVOCAL, and she had me dead to rights. It had taken me four years to get out of the gutter and another two to make real money. I could have come to her a hundred times, but it was never enough. I was nursing some old wound where I wasn't good enough. Never good enough.

So there I was. Not good enough because I'd waited too long to be good enough.

She was right there, over that little crest of land, behind the factory that had closed eleven years before.

Not waiting. I should have known. Why would she wait? It wasn't long after I left that she started dating Frank Marshall, the best-dressed kid in our grade. I should have given up on her then, but I couldn't.

I could go see her. Nothing was stopping me. She could tell me she didn't want me to my face. She owed me that.

She didn't.

Since Lance had been from Johnny's litter, I left him a message with the details. I didn't know if he'd even remember me.

The roses were being trimmed outside the club's café. An older man with a floppy hat covering his brown skin was doing an efficient and more than adequate job of it. I went in for an early dinner and took a table overlooking the bushes. A few flowers braved the autumn temperatures. Even through the glass, I could hear the *pock pock* of tennis balls.

I was a paper cutout of a sixteen-year-old boy, sloppily taped onto the page of his life thirteen years later. Or maybe I was the hedge fund manager tripping into the scene of a play he'd starred in as a boy.

"Chris Carmichael?" A woman in a navy suit stood over me with my Coke. She put it in front of me and folded her hands in front of her. She had a blond bob and fresh red lipstick. She looked nothing like the girl I'd known when I worked the grounds, but I recognized her anyway.

"Marsha!" I stood and shook her hand. She pulled me forward and embraced me. I pulled out a chair for her, and she sat. "I didn't think anyone would recognize me."

"Well, I didn't exactly," she said. "I saw your name in the registration log."

"Really?"

"I'm part owner here now, so I check it daily to make sure everything's taken care of. I couldn't believe it when I saw your name. How far you've come from biking all the way here from Barrington!"

"Yeah, and you." I indicated the breadth of the club. "Part owner?"

She waved it away. "It was invest in something or starve."

When we were kids, I'd thought people like Marsha had infinite resources, but as a man, I learned better. Anything could be lost.

"Good investment then."

She put her elbows on the table and leaned over her folded hands. "What brings you back?"

I'd come for two reasons, and both sounded ridiculous when repeated.

"My dog died. He was born here, so I figured I'd bury him here. Up at Wild Horse Hill."

"Aw, I'm so sorry." Her eyes flicked to my left hand. She was looking for a ring. I saw hers. The diamond was the size of a gumball. "My daughter buried her bunny up there."

"You have children?"

"Two by my first husband. Mattie and Oliver. You have any?"

"No." The shortness of the answer begged for clarification. I had nothing to lose by making conversation, except time. "Never got around to finding the right woman."

She laughed a derisive little laugh. "Had mine with the wrong man, but they turned out all right." She slid open her phone. "You remember Mitch Whitney?"

"That asshole?"

He wasn't an asshole. He was a solid guy who'd laugh at being called that.

"He's my second husband, and the right one. Charles…you remember him?"

I nodded. He was a real asshole.

"He knocked me up in that pool house right over there." She pointed out the window. The pool house wasn't visible past the courts, but we both knew where it was. She handed me her phone. The wallpaper was of a family on a boat with fishing poles cutting the sky behind them. Her, a man our age, and two kids. "Figured what the hell, right? Well, he was an a-hole all right. Wouldn't marry me. Said our son wasn't his up until the last minute. Took me five years to leave him, and his family made it hard. But I got out."

"And is this the new Mr. Marsha?"

Her face lit up like a Christmas tree, as if I'd brought up her favorite subject. I handed back her phone. "I met him and it was, like, I don't know. You ever play piano?"

"No."

"Well, I don't know how else to describe it, so you're going to have to live with it. You fight the metronome and then you get to this point where you feel the rhythm. And it's easy. The song flows through you like it's already there. That was what it was like the minute I laid eyes on Mitch. But you don't play music, so you don't know what that's all about."

"No, actually, I do."

"You play something else?"

"No. But do you remember Catherine Barrington?"

"I do."

It was too much to speak about. She'd nod sadly at my loss or we'd laugh about it.

"How is she?" I asked, sticking to the subject while I pretended to change it.

"Still living in that old house. Her dad closed the factory and died, I don't know, maybe ten and change years ago? Their mother took off and left those girls."

"What?" I had known the factory closed, but not the ugly personal details.

Marsha nodded. "The girls were of age and they had trust funds, but still. It was a tragedy. Catherine's like a saint now. Selling everything to keep the people in that town afloat."

Her letter got taut in my pocket, stretching the fabric to let me know it was there.

Please accept my condolences.
Sincerely,
Catherine

SHE'D NEEDED ME, and I'd let her down. I wasn't worthy of her or a warm welcome.

"It's her birthday, did you know?" Marsha said.

Did I? I knew it was in autumn because it was a few months after I left. It had taken me hours to find the right card and I'd skipped a meal to buy it. "I forgot."

"One of the Barrington guys who fixes the AC mentioned there's a party. You should show up." She winked. "Might be like playing music."

CHAPTER 19

CATHERINE

One thing you could say about the people of Barrington, they wouldn't know how to kidnap someone and hold them for ransom. They'd used one of Mrs. Boden's scarves to blindfold me and I could see right under it.

I was in front, with Juanita and Kyle guiding me down the hall and a crowd just behind them. Harper was up in her room with a headache but wished me a happy birthday from under the covers.

"I remember when this was unveiled the first time," Mrs. Boden said. She was over ninety and remembered everything from the past sixty years as if it happened at breakfast. "You cried the entire time."

I remembered too, and they weren't tears of joy.

"Okay, ready?" Juanita said.

I nodded.

The blindfold dropped, and everyone shouted, "Happy birthday!"

I was in the doorway of the room I'd occupied after Chris left, and it looked so bright and happy I had to squint. Flat cream walls. New moldings. Repaired sconces. Even the doorknobs had been polished. I looked up. The painted tin ceiling was still there, flying monkeys and all.

"Don't touch the walls," Kyle called from behind. "Not yet."

I turned to the crowded hall. "Thank you."

Two of the children were jumping up and down with tiny-toothed smiles. They didn't know why this room was significant to me. They only knew how to react to the happiness of others.

I held my hand out to Taylor.

He took it and said, "Let me show you what we did."

He showed me the new fixtures in the bathroom, the fixed and finished French doors. Mostly though, he proved the ceiling remained untouched. The monkey wings were there.

"That's all we could do," he finished. "But the floor needs to be done, and you need new pipes and a rewire."

"Can I sleep in it?"

"Paint should be dry by tonight."

My cheeks tingled because I knew they'd fixed it up because Chris was coming. I hadn't told anyone he wasn't and I hadn't told them that I didn't know if I was staying or going.

But they were happy. The barbecue was smoking, and children were playing in the yard like kittens. The dogs, including old Percy, the runt of the litter and its last survivor, nipped at their heels. The kitchen was a hub of activity with Trudy gossiping and her older sister washing the dishes. The guys joked with Taylor about his proficiency with a nail gun. I watched from the back porch as the town went about its business. It would do the same whether I was here or not.

"You all right?" Johnny asked, tipping his empty beer at me. He was in his biker vest and a long-sleeve shirt that showed the tattoos that snaked over the tops of his hands.

"I'm fine."

"You looked a little misty." He leaned into the cooler for another.

"Birthday mist." I heard the doorbell from the other side of the house. Weird. Everyone was coming around the driveway. "Let me get that."

Bernard beat me to it, opening the front door to a very tall and handsome man in a black button-front shirt. He had a bottle of champagne in his hand.

"Hello?" I said.

"Friend of Taylor," Bernard said. "I'll get him."

Rather than get him, the stranger took two steps to the base of the stairs and called up, "Hey! Hard-on!"

"Oh, I'm so sorry," I said to the tall man. "He's—"

"It's fine. I'm Keaton, by the way." He had a British accent. It was nice.

You can go to London.

"I'm Catherine. Come in."

I could go to London.

Not for long. I didn't have a ton of money. But they spoke English and I could get a job, or if I could find a buyer for the house, I'd have enough to live on for a while.

Taylor bounded down the stairs to his friend and I went outside. The sun was about half an hour from setting, and all my people had shown up after work or between shifts. They'd stay until the house was clean and the crickets were louder than the children.

I could leave them. They didn't need me. If that Silicon Valley tycoon came to buy the factory, it would again be the hub of the town. Some would work there, some would be disappointed, but the purpose of the little place would be established without me.

I looked over the family cemetery hiding under the wild thorns. Last week, Harper and Taylor had started cutting through it but stopped halfway through, at our father's headstone. I couldn't blame them. The tangle was thick and twisted, dangerous to touch, guarding the history and roots of the Barrington family.

If I left, what would happen to my ancestors?

Standing at the edge of the white fence bordering the thorn bushes, I put my hand on a thick branch. I was immediately stuck by a sharp pain in my palm. I let it cut me.

"Catherine," Reggie said from beside me, "you ain't wearing down the points like that."

"Maybe I don't want to wear them down."

"Maybe you don't."

He waited, and I drew my hand along the thorn, opening my skin. The blood falling on the branch looked black in the long shadow of the sun.

"This thorn bush," I said. "I let it grow to keep Harper from defacing the graves. And because I didn't want what was in here to be lost."

"You can talk without cutting yourself open," he said quietly. He must have thought I was going to slice my wrists on a thorn.

"I want to leave here," I said. "I want to go far away. But I can't."

"Why not? You think this whole town wouldn't put together the money for you to go where you needed?"

They would. I hadn't considered taking a penny from them and never would, but I knew they'd support me. Their wishes weren't the issue.

"And what would happen to this house if I sold it? My family's graves? My history? Harper's not going to be here much longer. There's no one. I'm the last Barrington standing. I'm trapped. I might as well be under these damned bushes. They might as well have grown over me the past thirteen years.

"I don't know how to get out. I don't know how to ask for help because it's not a thing or money in my way. It's me. I'm in my way. How am I supposed to get out of the bushes if the bushes are *me*?"

I didn't realize I was yelling and crying or that I'd attracted an audience.

"I don't want your pity," I shouted. "I love you, every one of you, but I want to get out of here now. Right. Now!"

"The bushes ain't you," Reggie said. "We're going to show you."

He walked off, passing Damon, put his hand on Bernard's shoulder and said something in his ear. They both sprang into action. Bernard said something to Orrin and Pat, who went to their cars. Damon reached under the barbecue for a can that—logically—could only be one thing.

"Now, here's what I want to tell you and everyone." Reggie popped the top off a gas can. "Catherine Barrington, get the fuck out of this shithole town." He poured gas on the bushes.

"Reggie!"

"What?" he said. "You wanna save this mess?"

Orrin waited with a silver can. Damon had his lighter fluid. Juanita hustled the kids away.

"You're drunk!" I said, referring to all of them.

"I'm asking you," he replied. "You wanna get rid of what's keeping you?"

Damon, a troublemaker since the day he was born, put an unlit cigarette in his lips, watching me like the rest of them. "Whatever, man." He squeezed a stream of fluid onto the thorns. "These bushes are ugly and you got to go."

They wanted me to leave.

I felt a little betrayed. I understood that they wanted me to be happy, but I wanted to be wanted more than I wanted happiness.

I was backward, and for the first time, I knew it.

So I nodded to Reg. For the sake of continuing something, anything in a forward direction, I motioned that it was okay to proceed. If I wanted my own life, I had to give up being needed.

I didn't know who threw the match, but it took all of a second for the entire thing to go up in flames. I got blown back a step by the heat and light, putting my arm over my eyes. It was big. As tall as the house and bright enough to turn off the light sensor bulbs on the porch, it raged so hot that it seemed like the end of everything. Nothing could continue as it was after a fire like this burned in my own yard. No part of my life would remain untouched, unchanged, or unbroken.

I was free.

I'd said it before, but I felt it in my heart when the thorn bushes burned.

I was free.

Was I smiling?

Part of my yard was on fire, Damon was lighting a cigarette in it, and I was smiling as if I had any business doing anything but panicking.

"Stand back!"

The clap of the screen door and the voice behind me were muffled by the roar of the blaze.

Still in a calm, fixated state, I didn't jump when a man in a jacket and slacks blew past me. He carried a fire extinguisher canister in one hand and held the hose in the other. I had no reason to recognize him. No one in town wore nice clothes to a barbecue, and the smoke and clouds from the fire extinguisher obscured his face.

I didn't need to see it.

"Chris!"

As if woken by Chris's command to stand back, Orrin jogged to the shed. Kyle ran for his truck. Taylor turned on the hose and soaked the porch. Four fire extinguishers on the blaze, my house wasn't going to burn down, and I was free to go anywhere in the world I wanted.

The world had turned upside down. Everything had fallen out. I'd been ready to refill my life with new things.

Then he came back a day early and put out the fire in my house.

He turned to face me, dropping his fire extinguisher with a *clonk*.

Where was the rest of the world before the moment our eyes met again? Before I saw that boy inside the man? He barely had scruff on his cheek when he left, and now? He had little lines around his eyes and a searing intensity that a boy can emulate, but only a man can achieve.

Missing the muscle and lithe movements that defined the Chris I knew, he'd become something harder, more solid, shaping the space around him instead of bending with it.

And still, he filled me.

Everything clicked into place all over again. I only heard laughter around me, as if every tension in the universe snapped.

I was free of commitments and free of plans. Free of any kind of ambition or hope. He walked right into the space those tiny things had taken up.

Which didn't mean I wasn't mad. I balled my fists up and got ready to give him hell, but he spoke first.

"I got your note."

He came close to me. Close enough for me to smell him past the burning wood and spent lighter fluid. Close enough to see the sweat on his cheeks and the way his lashes were slightly darker than his hair.

"I told you I couldn't see you." I must have been out of my mind.

"You made a mistake." He growled as if we hadn't spent thirteen years apart. As if I'd just seen him yesterday and he was responding to a text I'd sent an hour ago. As if we even knew each other anymore.

And we didn't.

But time had folded and bent around my feelings, coming to

the other side and wrapping us together again like a twist-tie. It really did feel as though we hadn't been apart at all. My experiences lied to me, and my feelings were deceptive. My senses fabricated rightness out of nothingness and what little sense I had was spun into a mess of conflicting information.

"Get out," I said, pointing at the door he'd come through. "Go through the house and out the way you came. Go home."

He tried to put his hands on me, but I curled inside myself and slunk away. If he touched me, I'd be lost.

"Catherine—"

"You can't do this, Christopher. You can't just storm in and act like you've been here for me the entire time."

A waft of leftover smoke blew between us. I blinked hard to keep it out, and so I wouldn't have to look into the eyes that felt like home.

"That's the past," he whispered.

No one came into our space, but I felt them watching. Listening. Making sure I was all right.

I wasn't all right. I was confused. I had thirteen years of hurt and disappointment built up. Crying myself to sleep had been a completely inadequate valve for what had built inside me. And the sorrow was nothing compared to the love eating it alive.

He was a mistake wrapped in relief tied with a bow shaped like everything I found beautiful.

Calmly, I walked past him, through the house, to the front door, and out to the quiet front yard where he'd stood thirteen years before and thrown a tennis ball at the wall outside my bedroom. When I spun, he was right behind me, and when I opened my mouth to speak, he planted a kiss on it.

I felt a hardness of spirit, a stern resolve against obstacles. A forward motion that drove his lips into mine, and I felt—from instant to instant—a crumbling in that rigidity. His body curved where it had been angled, his mouth went soft where it had been firm. His fingertips brushed my neck as if asking for things he'd gotten accustomed to demanding.

He was falling apart right in front of me.

We split apart to breathe. I gasped.

"Chris." I had so much to say, but only his name came out.

"I'm here now."

"So?"

"It's all over. I can fix this."

"Fix…" My face tingled, and I had to hold my hand in front of my mouth. He rubbed my shoulders. It felt so good to be touched like that. I'd been crying alone for so long, I'd forgotten what tender company meant. I swallowed it back to speak. "Fix what?"

He threw his hand out to the dark night. "All of it. I made it, Rin! Do you know what this means? All this is over."

My body was stiff and my mind stuttered. I didn't know whether to thank him or slap him, so I did nothing.

"I can tell," he said. "I can't believe it, but I feel the same, exactly the same. It's like a light went on."

He seemed happy. Relieved even. With the moonlight on his cheek and the stars glinting off the whites of his eyes, cast in darkness, his voice carried happiness and relief. A car came down the driveway, casting his face in harsh, moving lights. He looked like a man coming home after a long journey, and I was locked down inside my new ambition to move along with a life I'd delayed too long.

"I'm still in the dark, Chris. You left me. You left and you never came back."

"I'm back now. Do you remember? Right here in this front yard? The last time I saw you? It's like yesterday."

I was shocked back to life. "It wasn't."

His mood came down a notch. "It was the best time of my life."

"That's nostalgia. It's too late. You forgot me."

"I never—"

My hand shot up and covered his mouth. His face was rough with stubble and his lips were wet from our kiss. He felt more real and concrete than anything I'd ever touched, but he was a fleeting memory, a distraction. He'd hurt me badly enough to make me disavow the reality at my fingertips.

He kissed my palm, and taking my wrist in his hand, he kissed the tender skin inside it.

"Catherine?" Reggie called from the porch. "You all right?"

"I'll be in in a minute," I called to him, then faced Chris. "It's too late to ride in and rescue me. I don't need a knight in shining armor anymore."

"Maybe I'm the one who needs to be rescued," he whispered.

"I can't do that." I pulled my arm down, and he let go. "I'm sorry. I can barely save myself."

"Tell me you don't feel anything. Just say it."

I licked my lips, looking at the shadow of his, remembering the kiss. I felt something. I felt as if a long tether between us had been stretched to the limit and was suddenly pulled back. I felt a tight shell around us, woven in the hum of destiny.

"Say it," he repeated.

If I told him what I felt, what I knew to be true, my life would click into place like the last piece of a puzzle. Everyone wanted that. Everyone wanted to find their destiny and live it—except me.

I wanted to live a life I'd chosen.

I wanted to make my own mistakes.

I wanted my own suffering. My own joy.

"Say it," he whispered again, putting his face closer to mine. The porch light flicked on, and I could see the face that was so hard to resist. "Say what you feel."

I swallowed the truth and said what needed to be said. "I don't feel anything."

Chris's reaction was subtle but unmistakable. He blinked twice, flinching slightly as if slapped. I heard the wood planks on the porch creak. Reggie had stepped forward. He'd get between Chris and me if he had an inkling that I wanted him to.

I didn't want him to.

This, I needed to do for myself. Only I could break from my past, and staying in the front yard with the man who had left me all those years ago wasn't helping. I needed to rip off the Band-Aid.

"I'm sorry about Lance," I said. "I have to go."

I brushed past Reggie to go back into the house.

CHAPTER 20

CATHERINE

*S*adness and I were well-acquainted. It was a thickening cloud in the soul dispelled only by deep, genuine tears. It was a drop of oil in a glass of water that could only be thinned into tiny bubbles and, if left unchecked, would coalesce again into a slick ball of contamination.

Sadness felt like me, but a little heavier, a little thicker, a swarm of gnats I could dispel with a wave of my hand, only to find them massing around me again.

After everyone went home, leaving the house spotless and the thorn bushes charred and wet, I went to the suite and sat on my bed, waiting to feel the weight on my heart.

I didn't feel sad. Not in the same way I always had, diluting something that would concentrate again. The hopelessness was missing.

Chris had come, and I'd sent him away.

I wasn't angry at myself or him. I wasn't disappointed or let down.

Instead, I was confused. Seeing him had thrown me, not

because it felt uplifting or high, but because I was suddenly grounded.

A knock at my bedroom door was followed by Harper's voice.

"Cath? You in there?"

"Come in."

She came in and landed next to me, arms around me, crying uncontrollably.

"Harper! What happened?"

"Nothing."

"Where's Taylor? What did he do?"

"Shut up, okay? Just shut up."

She cried in my lap with her face buried in my thighs as I stroked her hair. I told her it would be all right, but I wasn't sure if it would be anything close to all right. Were we both going to be stuck here? Were we just looking for men to rescue us from ourselves?

I missed him. Chris Carmichael. I'd missed him and I'd continue to miss him the same way I missed who I'd been. I was too familiar with loss.

"You know what?" I said. "I was thinking of going to Europe. London, Paris."

"What happened to Chris?"

I sighed. "I chased him away."

A snap of a laugh escaped her as if she had a lot to say on the matter but didn't. "Why?" She sniffled. "Because you don't even know the guy?"

"Oh, I know him."

My sister didn't respond from my lap. She just folded her bottom lip until it creased.

"The minute I saw him, I knew him. I can't explain the connection, but my soul says he's as much mine as my own body. It's not sensible or practical, but in a way, it is. Gravity pulls down. Fire is hot. Chris and I are meant to be. It's almost boring."

She sat up. "Then why did you kick him out?"

Why had I? Because I had pride. I was a grown woman with my own heart's desire and even if he was that heart's desire, I was in control of my actions.

"Wrong question," I said. "He left. He never picked up the phone. He never wrote me. The question is, why would I take him back?"

"Because you guys were meant to be?"

"It doesn't matter. I'm my own woman now."

She shook her head so hard her hair flew around her face. She looked as if she'd eaten a lemon and been attacked by a hornet at the same time. "What? You mean you weren't before? All this wasn't your choice? You didn't de-furnish the house and drain the bank account because it was your choice?"

"It was but—"

"But nothing." She stood, freeing me to get up as well.

"Harper—"

"You." She poked my shoulder, backing me toward the door. It kind of hurt. "What are you talking about?"

"I'm confused, all right? I'm confused!" I choked back a sob. No. No more crying. "I don't know where I fit in. I don't know what I want. No one needs me anymore. The factory's coming back. You're leaving—"

"What are you talking about?"

"I'm not stupid. I know Taylor's going to take you away."

She deflated.

"What?" I said.

Her face collapsed like a window breaking. Her expression dropped and curled into an uncomfortable, red-skinned blubber. Tears came so hard they cleared her cheeks and landed on her chin.

"Harper? What?"

She tried to speak, but just made spit.

"Did he leave you?"

My confusion was replaced with purpose, and it felt good. My blood flowed with it. As if my sister could see the chemical change in me, she shook her head violently but was lost to sobs before she could get a word out. Her pain felt like a compressed version of the months I'd waited to hear from Chris.

I was angry. Very angry.

"I'm going to kill him. Nobody hurts Harper Barrington. Nobody. Do you hear? And not just me. Oh, no. You mark my words, every man in this town is going to make it their business to find Chris and—"

Her face knotted even tighter and I shook the bees out of my head.

"Taylor," I corrected quickly. "Find *Taylor*. Whatever. They're going to find him, and if I have to use every last dollar to send them to California, I swear to God—"

She grabbed me by the shoulders, still sobbing too hard to speak, and held me tight.

"I'm sorry, Catherine," she choked out. "No one's coming to buy the factory. It's done. We lost."

I stroked her hair. I didn't ask her how she knew. Harper knew things. The end.

We lay on my bed together under the mural of roses as she cried herself to sleep.

I was still needed. I should have been both sad and worried.

Instead, knowing I was needed and nothing had to change, I felt an immediate, guilty wave of relief. I shoved it under anger, covered it with disappointment, and hid it under a mask of resolve.

But the desire to maintain the status quo was there. Always there.

CHAPTER 21

CATHERINE

*J*ohnny's blue truck pulled into the driveway. He waved and got out wearing his yellow polo shirt. Redox slid out and came right up to the porch. The bruiser of a Rottweiler poked his nose between my legs one time to make sure it was me, then flopped onto the floor.

"Did you come for the grill?" I asked as Kyle got out of the passenger side.

"Yep." Johnny lowered the gate on the back of the bed. "Meat was pretty good last night. We nailed the timing on the evaporative cooling effect."

"Sure did," Kyle said.

My guess was that Johnny had worked out the equations to the half degree and Kyle had agreed to drink beer by the fire.

"You got coffee made?" Johnny asked me. "Been a long morning already and we have to bury Lance."

The funeral. Today. I'd told him I couldn't go and that was that.

"In the kitchen."

"Funny thing, Carmichael showing up last night."

Johnny stayed on the porch. Did he need an answer? Did he need me to say that I was skipping the funeral because I didn't want to see Chris or because I had a ton of chores to do? That I'd sent Chris away because I was confused or because I was empty? Because I was protecting myself from getting hurt again or from being happy?

"There's half and half in the fridge," I said.

He nodded and went into the house. I fell onto the porch swing, wishing this damn day would be over so I could think. Wishing Chris would disappear so I could decide if I'd made the biggest mistake of my life or dodged a bullet.

Harper was staying, at least for a while. I still didn't know the details of what had happened with Taylor, but he wasn't taking her away. At least not now. But she had to go. His presence had gotten me used to the idea that she should leave. I had time to convince her to go to college. Then once she got in, school wouldn't start until September. I could stay in Barrington a little longer.

If I wanted to.

I didn't know what I wanted anymore.

Johnny and Kyle came out with their travel cups and headed for the back. My eyes fell on the four mildewed boxes Taylor had left on the porch. I'd never bothered to take them inside. The crawlspace had not been kind to them. Maybe Johnny could haul them away on his way out.

I bent over the top box and used my fingernail to bend the flaps. Something shone from inside.

I decided to go all in. Sinks and soap were invented for curious hands. I opened the box all the way. The shine was from a glass doorknob that was probably one of the few made in the factory, along with a broken glass towel rack, a blue glass soap dish. Fancy hinges. A sconce. A door baseplate and a kitchen faucet.

I could sell some of it to the antique fixture place in Springfield. Some looked worthless. All of it was interesting. I didn't recognize any of it. It must have been Grandma's stuff from before the eighties, when Mom redid the house. Johnny would have things to say about what was in there; what had been made in the factory and what was worthless. He and Kyle were halfway down the driveway with the grill. I could ask when he was finished loading it.

I picked up the top box to lay it aside, but the bottom gave out and spilled the stuff all over. Well, that was just the kind of day this was. I got on my knees to clean up the mess before they ran over to help. I could do it myself.

A ceramic lamp base got stuck between the flaps of the box under it. When I pulled it out, the top opened. It was full of paper. Termites had made holes in the envelopes and left dust-sized wood chips all over the surface.

I put the lamp down.

The termites had eaten around the ink of the recipient's name, which was Catherine Barrington. They'd eaten around the postmark ink, which was New York, NY10005. They'd eaten around the return address label, which was a PO box in the same zip code, and of course the sender was Christopher Carmichael.

I flipped it over. The envelope had been eaten open, but the glue still hung on. It had never been opened.

Under it, another letter.

And another.

One fell apart in my hands.

Another was so black with mold, the address was unreadable.

None were opened.

All were to me, from Chris.

My hands shook so hard, I couldn't get my fingers in an envelope. I opened a folded piece of paper that fell out of an envelope. It was almost completely destroyed.

—I spilled coffee all ove—y pants I had but—you and—

I CHOSE ANOTHER. The ink had run when water hit it.

—Lan—in the dog park th—I hate to think he—nice guy. No guarantees of anything of c—and we can be together sooner rather tha— blooming because the flowers lie. You are the scent of roses—

I DUMPED the entire box on the porch and kneeled beside the pile. I went through it quickly, separating the readable from the unreadable.

—e getting used to—crowded but if you were with me b—everything—

—YOUR SKIN AND—HACKED at the tennis b—pleated skirt wa—one time in reality but in my—Frank Marsh—

FRANK MARSH—? Could that be Frank Marshall? The Christmas after Chris left, I'd started dating him. He'd begged me to, as a favor, and I stayed with him for his benefit and my own, until he finally came out of the closet. Mom had been devastated. I was happy for him.

—ny people. You'd li—used to i—re you getting these? Be—ove you,
Catherine of the Roses

I STOPPED SORTING them and searched for a whole letter. I couldn't
bear another minute. He'd written me and I'd ignored him. What
kind of hurt had he suffered because of me already? I needed to
know the exact height and weight of it so I could beat myself to a
pulp with his pain.

I opened one that looked relatively whole. A picture of Chris
and Lance fell out. He was kneeling next to the bloodhound, who
looked away from the lens at a squirrel or a pigeon or whatever a
loved dog looks at when his eyes are off his master.

The date was ten years before. Three years later, my father
died, my mother took most of the money and left. Harper stayed
home from MIT forever. I'd already stopped waiting to ever hear
from him again.

He was a cross between the hardworking, carefree, bronzed
boy I'd known that summer and the serious man who'd put out a
fire in my yard. The sun angled over his face, casting deep
shadows over one side and washing the other in white. His hair
was cropped and businesslike and his cheeks were smooth. Whatever transition he was making had been halfway over by the time
that letter came.

I sat on the porch rail and unfolded it. Most of the letters were
handwritten, some were printed. This one had his pointy scrawl
all over it. Had he written it at the dog park, or in the back of a
cab? I smelled the paper. Past the mildew from the box, I caught a
little bit of cologne, so I imagined him writing it at home, in the
morning before he went to work.

Dear Catherine,

It was as bad as I told you. I got everything out before the bottom dropped, but it was a scare. I was hoping to come back for you soon, but not now. I can't give you the life we agreed on.

But—and this is a big but—I have someone interested in a hedge fund that I've been pitching around. It's based in quantitative trading and something we call market inefficiencies (totally legal, I swear). I'll explain that to you when I see you. It's so safe and profitable, I'm sure I'm never going to come that close to losing everything again.

Which brings me to the same thing I end every letter with.

I hold on to you like I'm alone in the ocean and you're the last piece of wood from a shipwreck. What we had, I've never felt before or since. I belonged. I had purpose. You haven't answered a single letter, and I have no idea if you hate me or if your parents are hiding the stamps. I don't know if you're waiting or if you've forgotten me. My mother left Barrington months ago. If I come back, it's for you, but if you're finished with me, I don't want to know. I'm not ready to let go.

I'll keep on writing, but I have a bad feeling that one day I'm going to drown.

All my love,
Christopher

I FOLDED the letter but didn't put it back in the envelope. That would be like folding Chris up and putting him away. I couldn't betray him another time.

I read it again.

At some point before Mom left or Dad died, he'd written a last letter. It was in the box, shredded, damaged, or obliterated. He'd made a hundred, maybe two hundred, attempts to reach out to me and been ignored. He'd worked harder to contact me than I'd worked to forget him.

And my mother, or my father, or both had stopped the letters.

Or one had intercepted them and another had fought to keep them from being destroyed.

The only words they spoke to each other in those last years had probably been about those letters.

Was it too late to find him? Where was he staying? His mother's trailer was gone. The only hotel in Barrington, Bedtimey Inn, had closed years earlier. He didn't have any friends to stay with and Lord knows someone would have told me if he'd made plans to stay on their couch.

What was the difference anyway? Was I going to knock on his door and say, "Hey thanks for the letters," after I'd chased him away? And then what? Was I going to let him whisk me away like a knight on a white stallion? I still didn't know him. He wasn't the answer to my loneliness.

I put the photo of Chris and Lance in my pocket and looked through the two boxes underneath it.

Jesus.

More letters.

I owed him an apology, or at least an explanation. But it was too late. I was numb and I'd already sent him away. The letters would go into the trash with the rest of my mistake-filled life.

My foot landed on something soft and round. It rolled under me and I fell, dropping the box and landing on my wrists.

"Catherine?" Kyle and Johnny were loading the barbecue onto the truck, and Kyle dropped his end with a metallic clank.

"I'm fine." A yellow tennis ball rolled slowly away.

They were both off the truck. I held up my hands, but they helped me to my feet.

"You all right?" Johnny asked.

"Yeah. I stepped on a ball."

The culprit rolled to the porch step and Redox appeared, locking the tennis ball in his jaws. He came back and dropped it in front of me, sitting on his haunches expectantly.

I shook out my wrists, wiped my hands on my jeans, and picked it up.

"Yuck." It was slimy, but not everywhere. Still kind of new.

"Must be his," Johnny said. "Sorry about that."

"It's fine." I threw it into the grass and he chased it with the slow roll of a king who knows the ball isn't going anywhere. I fixed my hair and the guys went to strap down the barbecue.

With the hollowness still haunting me, I looked at my house as if for the first time.

What had Chris seen? Had he been disgusted by how I lived? The cracks in the paint, the missing shingles, the patchwork of roof tiles. I scanned the porch as Redox dropped the ball right in the letter box, as if he was done with this game. I was about to take it out, but the sad state of my house through a stranger's eyes was too horrifying to look away from.

The marks by the second floor window were still there from thirteen years ago, when a tennis ball had been thrown from the ground to get my attention.

He'd written to me. All of his feelings were lost to the elements, but he'd written to me repeatedly.

He hadn't abandoned me.

I'd abandoned him.

In a moment of vulnerability falling in a crack of time between breaths, my defenses fell away and the hollowness filled.

In that moment of opportunity created by a fracture in my armor, that old love I'd shut away saw an opening and took a chance, bursting through the fissure.

The feeling was like getting too close to a car moving at ninety miles an hour. I almost lost my footing. Emotions flooded me. They hurt like a too-rich bite of food early in the morning. It was urgent, heavy, and hot, an electrical current animating my body. Jacket. Bag. Keys. Box.

Sixteen.

I was sixteen. Smarter. More experienced. Twice as tired and half as ashamed, living from moment to moment, risk to risk, decision to decision.

Sixteen had been terrible, but the love had been real. It saturated my skin and laced my bones. His rightness. The click of the clouds and the sky locking together.

I ran back up to the porch and snapped a random letter from the nearest box, then I ran to my car.

"Catherine?" Johnny was strapping down the huge grill. "Are we blocking you in?"

"Don't worry about it." I got in and started the car. I had a quarter tank. "Johnny?" I called out the window. "Wild Horse Hill, right?"

"Yeah, we can go together."

Backing the car onto the lawn, taking down a hedge and a ceramic frog to turn, I drove around Johnny's truck and onto the driveway, avoiding their reactions in the rearview. I was sixteen again, and I only had the will to go forward.

CHAPTER 22

CHRIS

*T*he orange and yellow leaves up on Wild Horse Hill spun in cones when the wind whipped. Without close family, the holidays always approached with a certain stealth. There were no gifts to buy for kids, just sloshy parties in high rises. Glittering women and serious men returning to their true personalities under the influence of spiced drinks.

Lance had always been home for me, waiting for me to drop a tray of foil-covered leftovers in his corner of the kitchen. He'd been responsible for some of my best Thanksgiving memories.

In the front seat of the rental car, I scratched my head. A notepad leaned on the steering wheel, and I'd written only one incomplete line.

LANCE, you weren't just a good boy, you were—

WILD HORSE HILL was a disorganized mess of oddly-shaped tombstones from a hundred years ago to the present. The land had never been purchased for a cemetery, but no one in their right mind would buy it and dig up a bunch of bodies. The unofficial pet cemetery was behind a copse of trees. There wasn't as much of a view, but all the good girls and boys were at their master's feet.

—*YOU WERE FAMILY.*

SUCH A CLICHÉ. Everyone said that, but no one had a Lance. A car pulled up next to mine. Assuming it was the delivery guy with Lance's body, I got frustrated by the end of my time alone. I wouldn't finish the eulogy.

My irritation flipped to relief when the car's engine cut and I looked across the windows to the driver.

Catherine.

Jesus. Catherine. The girl in the roses. Not sixteen anymore, but filled out with experience and maturity. Knowledge made her even more beautiful.

Hold it together, Chris.

She got out, clutching her shoulder bag to her side, and stood at the front of her car with an envelope in her hand.

I got out. "Hi. I'm glad you—"

"I'm sorry."

"For?"

She handed me the envelope. It was desiccated and crumbling. The pale blue envelope I'd used to send resumes in had yellowed and browned at the edges. The envelope flap hung on by the last bits of glue. I looked at the front. Her address. My handwriting. We were at least joined in that.

"This was the last one I sent," I said, handing it back. I knew what was inside it.

"I didn't know," she said, clutching her bag's straps to replace her grip on the envelope. "My mother. Or my dad too. I don't know. She knew she was leaving as soon as she could, and she wanted me to be taken care of. She didn't want... me to make a bad choice. She hid them. All of them."

I looked at it again and flipped it open.

The night I met Lucia and she looked over my shoulder at my checking account, I'd been so broken about this letter.

"Did you read it?" I asked.

"No, I just pulled out one. There were boxes of them. All of them. I'm so sorry."

I handed her back the envelope. "Open it."

She took it and opened the folded paper. I hadn't forgotten what I'd written.

"Oh, Chris." She took out the check. "Seven hundred forty-nine."

I leaned over her to see my words.

We're even.

Just those two words in the center of a page. No more words of love. No more promises of one rose to the dollar or anything else. Simply an accounting.

"It was never about money," she said. "Not for me."

"I couldn't figure out what else. I couldn't believe you'd miss every single one."

"They must have hoarded them."

Catherine Barrington always saw the good in people. Thirteen years later, she was still defending her mother's paranoid psychosis. All I'd do by arguing was disabuse her of the illusions that kept her sane. I leaned on my car and she leaned on hers, the letter and the check fluttering in the wind as if they wanted to finally be free.

"If you'd read them, what would you have done?"

She looked into the wind, letting her hair blow away from her face. Her ear was perfectly shaped in a delicate swirl. The hole in her lobe was an empty comma.

"I want to say I would have run to you," she said, still looking over the cemetery. "I want to say nothing could have stopped me." When she turned back to me, her hair flew across her face like lines on a ledger. "But I don't know if I can say it. I never wanted to leave. Sometimes I thought I used you as an excuse to stay here. Then you were gone and I missed you, but would I have gone to you if I saw the letters? I don't know."

She pushed a pebble with her toe and I knew it was because she couldn't look at me. She was ashamed, and despite that, she was honest to her own detriment. With every word, she gave everything she had no matter how much it hurt her.

The distance between us wasn't more than two feet, but it was made of cold air and wind. Hard, black asphalt and the density of the years. I couldn't keep my hands away from her. I had to bridge time and the arm's length of miles between us.

When I laid my hands on her arms, she stiffened and looked at me.

"Do you want me to go away?"

"No," she whispered and relaxed into me.

I put my arms around her, and though coats and scarves and layers of fabric were between us, I could feel her heartbeat, the press of her fingertips on my back, and the rise and fall of her chest as she breathed.

"I wish I'd come," I said into her hair. "I was afraid it had been too long. But when Lance died…" I shook my head, struggling to put into words what he meant. "He was my last connection to Barrington."

"I wish I could have seen him." She pulled away enough to look at me. "Was he happy in New York?"

Was he? Had I ever asked myself that?

He was the harness that held me together. A bloodhound mutt

with floppy ears and a child's love was my connection to the boy I had been and the man I'd become. He was the reminder that I'd been a different man with a different future. He was the fork in the road. The opportunity to go back. The signpost away from loneliness and cold realities. Then time blew him away and I was left on a dark road disappearing into a point on the horizon. No more forks. No signposts.

But had he been happy?

He'd needed me and I'd needed him. That was all there was to it.

"He was a good boy." I barely had the sentence out before I choked back a sob.

Catherine said nothing. I held her tight and rested my head on her shoulder, crying for my lost friend and everything he represented.

CHAPTER 23

CATHERINE

I'd held men as they cried. They'd cried for lost babies and broken dreams. They'd cried for their self-image when their wives had to work. I'd held children with boo-boos and deeper hurts that would never heal.

All of that was practice for holding Chris in the cemetery parking lot. I took in his pain and made it my own. I was strong for him for just a moment. And I did something for him I couldn't do with anyone else.

I gave him hope.

I didn't mean to, because I wasn't sure what I wanted from him, but I became his last connection and his last hope. Hope for what? I didn't know. Nor did I know if I could shoulder the responsibility of it. He felt so good in my arms, and when I thought of him weeping without me, my jaw tightened with *no*.

He was mine to comfort.

The moment I accepted that in my heart, my mind rebelled. I was freeing myself. Now wasn't the time to go backward.

But his lips on my throat. His breath in my ear. His tears had stopped and the connection between us had started something else.

He paused when we were nose-to-nose, brown eyes so close I could see the flecks of black and green.

Could I do this?

"Don't kiss me," I said. "It's too soon."

"I won't." His lips brushed mine so gently, I only felt the shifting of air between us.

His gentleness forced me to yield, returning his kiss. He was different. The kiss was different. He was a little taller and broader, holding me tighter, and despite his vulnerability a minute ago, his kiss was confident. His kiss wasn't a demand or command. It listened, and my body screamed into it.

His kiss was achingly familiar, yet startlingly new. I remembered everything that I had tried to forget. I remembered the way his hands gripped my back as if trying to find purchase in the way his tongue could command my mouth, I remembered the feeling of a new beginnings. His kiss was the start of something old. His kiss was the birth of a child we knew and loved and welcomed.

"Chris," I said when I had to breathe. "Chris." I put my hand on his cold cheek.

He turned and kissed it, closing his eyes. "Do you forgive me?"

"Never. But also, I did the minute you came back."

"I want to go back and do it all again. Every moment."

We kissed again, but we weren't gentle. Passion excluded care, mouths slipping, tongues lashing to taste every surface in each other.

Gravel crunched on the road, and we pulled apart with an inward gulp as if we wanted to suck away the last of each other's breath.

Three trucks. Johnny and Kyle in the first. Orrin, Reggie, and Percy, who barked when he saw me, in the second. The black pickup in the back was strange to me.

Chris answered my question before I could voice it. "That's the delivery service with Lance." He straightened my collar. "The guys are helping me dig."

"I'll get you guys something to eat."

"Will you stay for the service?"

I'd forgotten I'd told him I couldn't make it. "Wouldn't miss it."

"Will you stand next to me?"

Orrin got out of the truck, and Percy jumped out, a smaller version of Lance.

"Yes," I said. "I'll stand next to you."

BY THE TIME I got back with coffee and sandwiches, the hole next to Galahad's plot was four feet deep and wide. A brown leaf fell onto Lance's black crate and surrendered to the wind, clicking across the surface and away. Percy sat next to it with his tongue lolling, standing guard as if he knew his brother was in there.

The men made short work of the job. Cross-legged like children, we ate and drank in the grass.

"How long are you in town?" Reggie asked Chris.

"As long as it takes." He tossed Percy a slice of ham from his sandwich and the dog kept his post while gobbling it up.

I knew what Chris meant, and I turned my face away to smile.

Reggie glared at the place where my knee touched Chris's. "Long as it takes to what?"

Reggie was a gentle man and an artist. He was one of us. But his voice dripped with alarming hostility and suspicion. Chris was going to answer and I had no idea what the reply would be. If he wanted to prove his commitment to me, he'd say he was staying for me. Or he could obfuscate. Or change the subject. But with his companion in a plastic bag, ready to be lowered into a hole, he might be vulnerable enough to make me his reason.

"Long as it takes him to bury Lance," I scolded. "And if he wants to visit with us afterward, he's as welcome here as anyone in the family."

Reggie snorted and wrapped up the last third of his sandwich.

Johnny, who was never good at letting things slide, threw a chip at him. "Take it easy, asshole."

"I'm easy. Sunday mornin' easy." Reggie got up.

"It's Friday, dumbass," Bernard said around a big bite of sandwich.

Reggie ignored him and pointed at Chris's feet. "Got your fancy shoes dirty."

"Yeah. Thanks for letting me know." Chris stood.

I gathered his trash before he had a chance to bend down for it. "We should get started before it rains." I picked up the last of the containers.

Above me, Chris reached down to help me up, but before I could take his help, Reggie was on my other side, offering his hand.

If I took Chris's hand, Reggie would lose his Sunday mornin' easy.

If I took Reggie's, he would get the wrong impression and Chris would feel betrayed.

With an armful of containers and foil, I only had one hand free.

I tensed it on the grass and got up myself without dropping a single thing.

"Let's get to it then," Johnny said, groaning about his bones creaking.

Kyle and Bernard followed suit. They lowered the black bag into the ground. I stood next to Chris as dirt clapped off it and Lance slowly disappeared.

"I have this thing," he said, taking out a leather-bound pad. "A few words. It's not very good."

Reggie scooped dirt into the hole and watched me with Chris. Was he going to be a problem? I didn't think I could take it.

"Go ahead." I put a reassuring hand on Chris's arm. He needed me more than Reggie did. "Please."

Chris ran his fingers through his hair. I'd never imagined him feeling insecure or unsure, but the cracks in his confidence were wide enough for me to see what was inside him.

The boy I'd loved.

He looked at the paper, then back at me. I nodded, loaning him a little confidence.

"Lancelot Carmichael, you were a good boy. Always. You were always there for me, even when I didn't have food for you."

He stopped, tilting the paper. That was all that was on it, but he kept going.

"When it was raining and cold, he stayed with me." Chris closed his book. "He gave me everything. There was this one time, right in the beginning, when I had..." He made a rectangle with his fingers. "I had this much in a Chinese food container. It was all I had. I knew he was hungry, but when I offered, he wouldn't take the meat. He pushed it to me. He took care of me, even when I failed him... and... I'm sorry, Lance. I'm sorry for letting you down. Putting you second to my work. I'm so sorry."

His fingers found mine. We twined them together, and he squeezed my hand so hard I thought they'd fuse into a single gesture.

He let go and helped shovel dirt in. When it was no longer a hole but a mound in the grass, we set up the slab of stone at the head.

Lancelot Carmichael
Brave Knight.

146

Marked territory in Barrington and New York City
2004-2017

Chris held my hand on the way back to the car. He leaned into me and whispered, "Tonight. Are you free?"

"Lucky for you, I am."

"Can you meet me at our tree?"

I couldn't contain my smile.

Reggie watched us from the other side of the parking lot, and he didn't look happy.

CHAPTER 24

CATHERINE

I discovered the picture of Chris and Lance in New York in my pocket and inspected it. It was taken early in our separation. The background was hatched with monkey bars, blurry children running, a chain-link fence with a solid wall of red brick behind it. The ground was beige concrete. Lance was fully grown, looking away from the camera. Chris was still a boy, and very much a man. His shirt was tight in the arms, his pants were short, and he crouched next to a knapsack that had seen better days.

I flipped the picture. He'd handwritten the date and a note.

We miss you.

"I MISSED YOU TOO."

What had I been doing when this picture was taken?

Against the back wall of the hall closet, I kept a stack of photo albums. I kneeled on the floor and fingered the spines, plucking out one of the middle. Hunched in front of the closet and opened it in the middle.

My world had red brick in the background too. The factory closed. Daddy had given notice two weeks before, and the workers had set up a "locked doors party" onsite, celebrating what they couldn't control. It had seemed like a bump in the road back then. Something to have a few beers and eat barbecue over.

I put the picture of Chris and Lance in that timeframe.

Downstairs, something shattered. I hurried to the kitchen to find Harper cleaning up a broken glass in bare feet.

"Are you all right?" I pushed her away, taking the broom and dustpan. Her hair was greasy, her eyes were puffy, and her lips were bitten red.

"I'll get over it." She hoisted herself onto the counter and got a new glass from the rack. She filled it, sniffling.

My sister didn't cry. I did all the crying for the family. Harper worked, studied, followed her curiosity down rabbit holes. Her spirit had been crushed. Something beautiful had been destroyed. I jammed the broom into the corners and edges of the kitchen as if I wanted to beat the glass out of them. My rage had its own mind, running my blood faster and hotter, contracting my muscles into tight, sinewy braids.

"Where is he?" I asked, slapping the edge of the dustpan into the trash. The glass tinkled in.

"He went back to California," she said into her glass before she finished it, looking out the window. "It's over. I have things to do now." She put the glass on the counter and saw me for the first time since I walked in. She put her hands up as if warding me off. "Whoa, Cath. It's okay."

"It's not okay."

"I've never seen you look like that."

"Like I could kill him?"

"Yeah."

"I will. I'll fly to California and find him and rip him apart." I wasn't going to kill him. I wasn't going to shred him. But I wanted to, and I could get close enough by saying it. "Look at you. You've been *crying*."

"You cry all the time."

What a sad, sad accusation.

"It's a tension release. You're crying over Taylor leaving, and I'm going to kill him."

She picked her glass up again and filled it. "It's not his fault. I broke up with him."

"Why? You liked him."

She took a long drink. "I love him." Her face scrunched as if she was ready to cry all over again. "But he was ready to give everything up for me, and I can't live with that. I can't live with holding him back."

She broke down in tears, slipping off the counter and into my arms. I took her glass and put it safely on the counter while holding her. My beautiful, genius sister. The one who was supposed to go anywhere and do anything, she felt unworthy enough to be unhappy rather than bring someone else down.

"You wouldn't have, Harper. That's…" The idea was absurd, ridiculous, unjust. I kissed her head as it shook against my shoulder. "Are you wiping your nose on my shirt?"

She nodded against me. "I have to do laundry anyway."

I gave her a paper towel. She took it and stepped into another hug. I stroked her hair and leaned against the counter while she sniffled in my arms.

"Can I tell you something you don't want to hear?" I asked.

"No."

"You need to finish college, Harper. Not to make yourself worthy, because you're the best woman I know. But because you need to be the person you were meant to become. I did it here. You can't. The world needs you to do that."

She leaned away from me, leaving me with an empty, cold place where her sadness had been. She honked into the paper towel and folded it in half so she could blow her nose again.

"The world needs you too," she said, sniffing and wiping the sides of her nose.

"Maybe." Outside, a car pulled down the driveway. "But you need to think about college again."

"I will."

We both looked out the window. Reggie's Chevy was driving so slowly into the garbage cans that they tipped but didn't fall before he stopped the car.

"What is he doing?" Harper asked.

I looked at the clock. It was only ten minutes after noon. "I think he's been drinking."

I went out the side door before Harper could reply.

Reggie got out, letting the door open so hard it bounced halfway closed again as he came toward me like a man barreling into a bar fight.

"Reggie!"

He put his hands on my face and his mouth on mine. He tasted like beer and desperation, and when I pushed him away, he grabbed me tightly so I couldn't get away.

The *klonk* was preceded by a whiff of wind and followed by Reggie's grunt. He was off me, and Harper stood a foot away with the top of a metal garbage can in her hands. Reggie had been thrown against the side of the house, bleeding from the head.

"Jesus!"

"Don't you do that, Reginald," Harper shouted. "I'm mad enough to take you out, drunk or not."

Reggie's response was a series of sharp ahs and moans. He stumbled trying to get up. "Why'd you do that?"

"If I gotta tell you..." Harper wielded her garbage can cover like a knight carried a shield.

"I was just trying to…" He took his bloody hand away from his skin. "Jesus."

"I'll get you some ice," I said, still tasting his beer on my tongue.

"It's bleeding!"

"And a towel."

"Catherine, you know I didn't mean anything by it, right?"

He came toward me, but Harper got her backswing ready, turning the shield into a weapon.

"You're drunk." I started for the side door.

"You want his money, don't you? You think he can take care of you."

I didn't have to answer him. I didn't owe him an explanation of my feelings or actions.

"Sit down, Reggie." Harper swung a plastic chair behind him. "Before I give you a concussion, sit."

He ignored her. "He can't. You know he lost all his money right? He's got nothing."

I felt a few things at once.

I was sad for Chris. I knew how hard he'd worked.

But it didn't reduce my attraction to him. It increased it.

Why?

Why would it even matter?

Leaving the side door behind, I stood in front of Reggie and pushed him gently into the chair Harper was holding still.

"Reginald, I'm sorry you feel rejected. I know it hurts. I hate that you're hurt and I hate that I hurt you, but I don't hate it enough to lie to you. Don't kiss me again. Ever. Drunk or sober. Ever. I'm going to call Johnny to bring you home."

I stomped into the house, and Harper was right behind.

Before the door closed behind her, Reggie shouted, "You're a whore, Catherine Barrington. A fucking whore!"

"Oh, fuck this," Harper started back out, but I grabbed her arm.

"Leave him be." I closed the door and locked it. "He'll regret it when he sobers up whether you concuss him or not." Picking up the wall phone, I dialed Johnny and Pat's house.

"He did, you know," she said while the phone rang.

"He did what?"

"Chris's hedge fund lost a bunch of money. Something like seventy-three point four six percent of its value."

"I don't care."

"I mean, guys like that are never totally broke. He probably has a billion hidden away."

"Still don't care."

"Hello?" Johnny's voice came over the phone.

"Hey, Johnny, are you on shift this afternoon? Reggie needs to get picked up and poured into bed."

Johnny agreed to fetch him. I hung up and prepared an ice pack.

Someone was going to deeply regret kissing me, and I wasn't sure who.

CHAPTER 25

CHRIS

*M*arsha's office was bright white, bedecked in fresh flowers and sunlight. I sat on the white-leather-and-chrome chair, and she sat across from me. Elbows on her white wood desk, she steepled her fingers. She had two huge rings on each hand and matching bangle bracelets. Her right eye squinted in my direction, and that side of her lips curved into a smile.

"We all had a feeling you two went back there," she said.

"Grounds keeping had its privileges."

"And you need it set up by tonight?"

"I'll pay for the service and tip whoever has to do extra work to get it done."

"You bet you will."

"I need access and privacy."

"We aim to please, Mister Carmichael."

We shook on it. As she led me to the door, she said, "She's worked hard for everyone else over there. It's nice to see something good happen to her."

"I may not be all that good."

154

"At least Harper won't have to hit you over the head." I must have taken too long trying to put her meaning together, because she explained without me having to ask. "You didn't hear?"

"I just saw her." What possibly could have happened?

"Gossip travels fast around here."

She untangled the grapevine on the way to reception. Reggie had gone to the Barrington house to make Catherine his, and when she refused, Harper had done something completely expected and bashed him over the head.

I made light of it, and Marsha promised to have the club set up for me by nightfall.

Everything was going fine, but it wasn't. It was terrible. I didn't know how long I stood in that front garden, staring through a rosebush, asking myself what the hell I was doing. I'd disrupted everything.

A bit of yellow was visible at the base of the bush. I reached through the leaves and thorns. A tennis ball. You were supposed to throw it back, but no one was playing nearby. The kid who kept the grounds would take it back to the pro shop and toss it in one of the coach's baskets.

The pro shop window was manned by a young woman in her teens. I held out the ball.

"Can you toss this in a basket?" I asked. "I found it in the garden."

"They're locked up. You can keep it or leave it here."

I put it on the counter. "Is Irv around?"

She looked puzzled. "Irv?"

"He was… who's the manager?"

"Oh! You mean the last manager? He died in…" She counted on her fingers.

She told me the year, but it didn't register. Irv was dead. The guy who'd given all the poor kids jobs. The guy who'd witnessed my first kiss with Catherine. Gone. And I didn't even know. I should have known.

"Sir?"

"Right. Well." I took the tennis ball off the counter. "Thanks for your help."

I walked back to my car in a fugue, clutching the yellow ball in my fist.

No matter what happened in Barrington, no matter how I walked away, no matter how long I stayed, or my success on a mission I couldn't even define, I couldn't leave things worse than when I came. I couldn't leave things undone, unsaid, broken.

I had to face Catherine about everything, and I had to face the town I'd abandoned.

Nothing about Barrington was the same as when I'd left, but maybe some things hadn't changed. On a Friday afternoon, payday, anyone who wasn't working would be at Walter's for burgers, beer, and pool. Or not.

I drove there on autopilot. Walter's still didn't have a sign out front, and the parking lot still smelled sour and dusty. Johnny's motorcycle with its sidecar sat in the lot out front, next to Kyle's prized Harley. I parked next to Orrin's pickup truck.

When I walked into the dark room, I felt like an outlaw riding into town. Conversations stopped, but the pool balls continued to roll and click. Faces were lost in shadow. Sunlight shot through the windows, bounced off the dust in the air, and was smothered in darkness before it could brighten the room.

I felt something warm and wet on my fingers.

Percy was licking them. I kneeled and rubbed behind his ears.

"Look who's buying the next round!" a young voice shouted. It was Damon. When I'd left, he was in fourth grade. I shook his hand.

"You don't need no more rounds," Orrin said, leaning on his pool cue.

"They still make burgers here?" I asked.

"Yeah," Johnny said from the bar. "But the fryer's been busted, so we get potato chips with it."

When I shook his hand, I saw Reggie at the other side of the bar with a rectangle of gauze attached to his forehead with a hashtag of tape. I slapped Butthead on the shoulder and gave Kyle a manly hug.

"Thanks for coming this morning," I said.

"Shouldn't be such a stranger."

I ordered a burger, and a beer appeared in front of me. I flipped a credit card on the bar and made a circle with my fingers, indicating I was indeed buying the next round.

I wished I'd worn jeans. I was casual in a sports jacket and button-front shirt, but I should have worn a T-shirt. Sneakers, not shoes. Or work boots that I didn't own, worn at the right foot, with a history of their own.

"Really, thanks for coming," I said to the bar at large.

"Had to watch Catherine," Johnny said. "Make sure you weren't going to take advantage."

"Thanks for that too." I sipped my beer.

The pool game resumed, and though I didn't expect Reggie to shake my hand or even greet me, he seemed isolated at the other side of the bar.

"What's up with Reg?"

"His head got in the way of an object at velocity. Mrs. Boden taped him up. She was a nurse in the Korean War. Didn't take no whining or crying from him," Johnny said.

"Should he be drinking?"

"A concussion woulda set him straight. But here we are."

Johnny wasn't going to tell me what happened, and I wasn't going to admit I already knew. I wasn't one of them anymore.

"Here we are," I said.

"When you going back?" Butthead asked.

"I don't know."

"We're pretty proud of you around here," Johnny said.

Butthead huffed. "He's the only one who understands what the fuck you do."

"Quantitative trading ain't that hard, asshole." Johnny turned to me. "Ain't hard to *understand*, I mean. If *doing it* was easy, this dimnut would have the scratch to drink imported beer."

"Fuck that," Butthead said. "Buy American."

"See what I'm saying? Get the fuck out of here while you can," Johnny said to me. "Place makes you stupid. I'd rather watch you make money from afar."

"What about Catherine?" I asked impulsively. I was tired of beating around the bush. "What if I took her away?"

"You got my blessing."

"Everyone south of the train tracks would shit bricks," Butthead added.

"You're south of the tracks, shithead," Johnny mumbled. "What are you going to do the next time you can't get antibiotics for your little girl? What are you gonna do when she's not here to feel sorry for your dumb ass?"

"She's done enough already. If people don't have their shit together, fuck 'em. Goes for me too."

The bravado wasn't lost on me. I'd entered adulthood with it. Walking into the biggest city in the world with a few hundred dollars in my pocket, ready to take over the world if that was what it took to win a woman I didn't understand. I'd thought money was important to her, but it wasn't. Never had been. Her people were important to her. Her tribe. I'd missed the point entirely.

I made eye contact with Reggie. He was still alone.

"I still love her," I said to Johnny quietly. "But I don't want to just come in here and cause trouble for anyone."

"Trust me." Johnny put his beer down with a deliberation that was punctuation. "We wouldn't let anything happen to her she didn't deserve one way or the other. But times are changing. Time she did too."

"What about you?" I asked as my food came.

He launched into his kids. They'd gone to college and never come back for more than holidays. One thing that came through his story was how proud he was of that exact fact. They'd moved on.

"You miss them?" I asked.

"Every damn day." With a tip of his chin, he ordered another beer. "Reg looks like he's gonna have an aneurysm."

He looked fine to me, but I had to trust Johnny on that. I took my beer and left my seat, crossing from the cool kids' table to the doghouse.

"Hey," I said, sitting next to Reggie.

"Fuck off."

There was no reason to answer him, but I wasn't walking away either. Not yet. I finished half my beer before he spoke again.

"She needs someone who isn't leaving."

"Yeah."

"Someone who appreciates her. Who isn't thinking she's someone she isn't."

"You should know."

In my complacency, he had me by the collar and pushed against the wall in a second. He was an artist and I was a mathematician, but the threat of a bloody fistfight seemed very real.

"She's not decoration," he said through his teeth. His eyes were lit by inner fire and his breath was soaked in beer.

Hands appeared on his shoulder. Kyle. Curtis. Johnny, of course. They pulled him off me, but his grip had never been the primary tools of attack. Our eyes were locked like two pit bulls in a ring. I wasn't letting him get pulled away any more than he was allowing it.

"You took your shot, Reggie," I said.

"She's not sixteen anymore. She's stronger than any of us. And your money? She's better than every single dollar you got. We all know it. This whole place rides on her back." He shook off the men holding him. They let him go but stayed close. "Well, I admit it, and I want to do for her. Take care of her. That's nothing for you, but it's something for me." He jabbed his chest hard enough to bend his finger back.

This felt like an extension of my conversation with Johnny and Butthead, but with a little more fire, a little more passion, and a single sentence that shook me.

We all know it.

I'd assumed, without thinking clearly about it, that I could take her away to something better.

But what did *better* mean?

I'd always thought it meant money, but what would have happened if I'd come for her? If I'd arrived on a white horse, rescuing her when I would have actually been rescuing myself? She wouldn't have become the woman she is. She wouldn't have been forged into the patron saint of Barrington.

I went to New York to make a ton of money, because I had to do that before I realized it wasn't important. If I'd stayed here or come back early, would I ever have understood that? Would I have come to that conclusion at Catherine's expense? Would she have come to represent everything that would have been wrong with me?

Worse, would I have spent the rest of my life chasing a dollar because that was what I'd been told I was worth?

"I fucked it up," Reggie continued, throwing himself back in his seat.

"Get up," Butthead said. "I'm taking you home."

Reggie kept on. "Fucked it bad, but that doesn't mean I'm going to just let you have her." By the last three words, he was shouting.

"It's not up to you. Or me."

Johnny put his hand on my shoulder. "You oughta go."

"You love a saint," I said, ignoring Johnny. "But she's not a saint. She's a living woman."

"You love a sixteen-year-old heiress. She's not that anymore either."

He was right. I'd come here hoping to meet the girl I'd left, but that girl was gone forever. She had been replaced by a woman of greater stature and purpose than I'd had the mind to wish for.

"I'm going to fight for her." I pointed in Reggie's face. "Don't underestimate me."

Johnny pulled me away. Reggie shook his head and let him take me outside. The sun was low in the southern sky and the afternoon wind rustled the dry grass. Everything was quiet, but nothing was still.

"Do you need a lift back?" he asked when the door shut behind me.

"Nah. Half a beer. Fuck it. Fuck it all. If I have to bulldoze over that guy or anyone for her, I will."

"Let him cool off. You'd do well to do the same." He handed me my credit card wrapped in a sales slip. "I grabbed this on the way out."

"Tell me something." I took a pen from inside my jacket and leaned on the wall to sign for the round. "Am I stealing her? Do they have something?"

"In his mind."

"And hers?" I handed him the signed receipt, and he snapped it away.

"If she says there's nothing, I believe her. She's not playing games, far as I can see."

After a shot in the arm, I was left alone in the parking lot.

CHAPTER 26

CHRIS

*a*t seven o'clock, I picked her up at her house. We exchanged ritual pleasantries and I held the car door open for her. When we were on the road, I tried to hold her hand, but they were tightly folded in her lap.

"Reggie came by today." She was turned toward the window and I was watching the road, but our attention to inattention was intense.

"I went to see him when I heard."

"You heard what?"

"That he made a pass at you and Harper clocked him." I couldn't look at her for long or I'd wreck the car, but she was worrying me. "I made sure he wasn't holding any grudges."

"Was he?"

"Only against me. Is everything all right, Rin? You said you didn't have a thing with him, but I can turn around right now if you want."

"No. There's nothing. Harper said you lost everything? All your money?"

My money? Was that what she cared about? Was she another

Lucia? Was she in my car because she thought she could make a killing? Would she bolt as soon as there was a whiff of trouble?

No. Not Catherine. I wouldn't believe that of her. I was more experienced in the ways of gold-diggers than I wanted to be, but I wasn't that jaded yet.

"I lost a lot."

"I'm sorry what you worked for all those years was lost. Can you make it back?"

I shrugged. "With a lot of effort, a change of strategy, probably. I just don't know if I want start all over."

"That's terrible."

"Maybe. Maybe not." I reached for her hand, and she let me take it. "I have other things to work for now."

THIS TIME, we went to the patch of grass just outside the fence legally, through a gate on the easternmost side that Marsha had loaned me the key for.

The tree we'd climbed in our sixteenth summer was wrapped with tiny white lights, and lines of hanging lanterns were strung between the fence and the branches in smile-shaped spokes. Garland and tinsel sparkled in the light.

Catherine stood right under it in the soft yellow light, looking up into the dense branches. "It's beautiful."

Her eyes were spots of glittering glass and her smile was brighter than any electric light.

"You're beautiful." I touched her face. I couldn't help it. "Want to climb it?"

"Sure."

I led her to the base of the trunk and put my hand on the bottom rung of my ladder. The bark had grown over some of the wood slabs, making the connection stronger but more treacherous since it was harder to get a foothold. "It's higher, so I might have to help you up. And you have to be careful to make sure your foot's securely on it."

She put her hand on the bottom rung where the bark had grown over. It was chest high.

"Here." I held out my hand. "Take a step back, kick up, and I'll get you on."

She understood me right away, kicking her right foot until it reached the lowest rung. I pushed her forward and up.

She took the next rung and looked down at me. "I'm wearing pants this time."

"I didn't look up your skirt last time either."

She climbed, taking the same path she had thirteen years earlier, scooting down the thick branch so I had room to sit. She swung her leg over so both feet were hanging over the same side. I straddled the branch so my chest was at her right shoulder.

"This seemed higher up when we were kids."

"It's only about eight feet." I kissed her cheek, lingering on her smell. Roses. Still roses. When she faced me, I kissed her lips, but after a few moments, she stopped.

"How did you leave it with Reggie?" she asked.

"I told him I was going to fight for you."

She leaned away from me. A string of lights blinked off, then on again, leaving a layer of darkness on her face.

"Did you?"

I leaned away only enough to catch her perplexed expression. "Yeah, I said that."

"No." She shifted a little, putting more of her right leg on the trunk. "Did you fight for me? When I was here, by myself, holding everyone in Barrington on my shoulders? Did you fight for me?"

I was defensive and I didn't know why. "Whoa, there—"

She wasn't going to be held up. She wasn't a horse with reins I could pull back. She was a tidal wave.

"You know—" She shook her head quickly, mouth tight as if she was trying to hold back a torrent. "I thought I was okay with this but no. No, I'm not."

"Catherine—"

Her name, or my voice, broke a dam for her. "Did you come? No. Did you check on me? Did you call? You knew my parents died. You knew the factory closed. You sat in your ivory tower in New York and turned your back, and now that you're divorced and you've lost everything, you think you can come back and tell Reggie you're going to fight for me?"

"I wrote you a hundred letters!"

"I didn't respond to a single one and it never occurred to you I wasn't getting them?"

"Oh, you know what, lady—"

"You had to know something was wrong when I didn't write back!"

"You got with Frank Marshall the minute I left!"

She sat in shock. The string of lights shorted again, blinking twice.

"My mother still lived here. She told me. And it hurt, but I kept writing. When you didn't write back, I figured you married him or—"

"Frank Marshall is gay, you stupid, stupid man!"

"What? You…" I couldn't finish the sentence. I had too many questions, but I didn't want to ask them. I wanted to yell. I wanted to defend myself against her accusations.

She was wrong. She had to be wrong, because I was nursing my own hurt. I couldn't be the one who was wrong. There had to be some way to turn this around, some way I didn't abandon her.

Her voice didn't soften. Anger clipped every word. "He needed a cover for a relationship he was having. So we 'dated' and my mother stopped trying to set me up with 'acceptable' young men."

"How was I supposed to know?"

"You could have asked. You could have picked up the phone. Come around once you had enough money. Sent your number with a sympathy card when Dad died. But you didn't. You're not going to fight for me, Chris. Don't lie to Reggie. Don't lie to me, and don't lie to yourself."

She straightened her back and let her bottom slide over the branch. Thinking she was going to fall, I took her arm to steady her.

"Let go."

"I don't want you to fall."

"You were supposed to go first so I could get off first, and you didn't. You forgot." Her tears dropped like summer rain, and her chin quivered like rose petals in the breeze. I couldn't deny I'd forgotten I'd said that our first time up in the tree. I could only sit still. "So much time's passed, bark's grown over the ladder, but when you said you'd fight for me, it all came back. It's like yesterday. This raw place where I know I'm not worthy of coming back to. I'm not worth fighting for. I'm shit."

"Cath—"

She was gone, pushed off the branch, landing on her feet, knees bent, arms out for balance. Looking up at me, the dots of light glint off her tears.

"You're not shit." I wished I could eat those words, because they're the bare minimum and she deserves the maximum. They're a denial, not a declaration.

"I know."

I dropped to the ground, but by the time I hit the grass, she'd already run away.

CHAPTER 27

CATHERINE

I'd meant what I said about the raw place, but the words I'd used didn't do it justice. It was a picture in my head, a taste in my mouth, a deep throbbing beat in my ears. I felt that raw place throbbing pink, pulsing with anger and self-loathing. It was where I was powerless and the place I'd tried to forget all those years. The only thing that silenced the throb and washed away the taste was sealing away other people's raw places.

I was aware that made a decade of philanthropy selfish and vain, but it was the only way to soothe my own hurt.

The garden path was dotted with lights on either side like an airplane runway. I'd been defying gravity for years and I'd suddenly skidded to the earth.

I heard Chris running behind me. I couldn't outrun him and I didn't want to. He caught up, came slightly in front of me, and turned so I could see him.

"You said you hadn't thought about me in years."

"What do you want me to say? That I had? Or that I hadn't? What's going to make you feel better?"

"What's going to make *you* feel better?"

I wanted to punch him and run into his arms. "I stopped waiting for you." I articulated each word as if that would keep me from being misunderstood. "I never forgot how you made me feel."

He took half a step toward me with his hands out, assuming he knew what I meant. He didn't.

"You made me feel worthless and forgettable. And I know it was all a misunderstanding, but that was how I felt. You can't take that away from me, because I carry it everywhere. But also..." I sighed.

My words bent him. Shoulders drooping, hands retreated to his sides, he looked damaged and small with his own exposed, raw places.

"But also..." I continued. "You made me feel loved and whole. I felt passionate and alive, and no one I've met since has made me feel like that. So I don't... I don't know what to do. I want to seize this thing with you and never let it go, and I want to throw it away to save myself."

"If I'd stayed, you wouldn't be who you are. I don't know how this will sound, but who you are makes me ashamed of who I've become."

"Who is that? I don't even know."

He paused as if gathering strength to confess a sin. "A man obsessed with money, and not sense enough to be ashamed of it."

I started down the path but slowly, inviting him to walk next to me. He fell into line and we walked shoulder to shoulder.

"In my line of work, we solve problems in the stock market and we use these processes called algorithms. They—"

"I know what an algorithm is."

"You do?"

"Harper rubs off on people."

"Right. So we use them to assess risk. How much to invest. Where to invest. How long to hold, when to sell. It can get complicated, but they work until they don't."

"Is that what happened to your hedge fund?"

He took a long time to answer, walking slowly. "What happened to the fund was that I changed the weighting. I weighted the making money too far over the potential loss, and I made bets without enough data. The scale tipped. And the more I think about it, the more I wonder if I did it on purpose."

"Why would you do that?"

"Because maybe I knew I needed to be completely miserable before I came back to my roots, and you."

"It wasn't about me, Chris. Don't say that."

We passed though the garden gate, toward his car.

"I can't help but think you were the last person who loved me for me. No more and no less. I weight that pretty heavily."

"I'm just an algorithm then?" I tried not to sound as if I was accusing him of something, because I wasn't. I was egging him to talk more.

"We all are, but we kid ourselves into thinking we have enough data to run it." We got to the car, and he unlocked it. "You make me feel like a man with a chance. You made me feel like that when I was sixteen, and I feel like that right now. With you, my future is mine to write, but I need more data. And so do you."

"You sure know how to make a girl feel all warm and fuzzy."

"The lights on the tree didn't work, so I recalibrated." He opened the passenger door.

"They worked. That's why I reacted the way I did." I got in the car before he could answer.

We didn't talk much on the drive back to my house, but as he got off at the Barrington exit, he grabbed my hand and held it. I let him, because his grip was exactly what I needed.

He walked me up the porch.

"I'm sorry I ruined your surprise," I said. "It was beautiful."

He slid his hands down my arms and linked his fingers in mine. "I should have come back. Fuck Frank."

"You can't. He's married to a nice guy in San Francisco."

My resistance was no match for his smile.

"I took years from you," he said. "We could have been together. I could have taken you back to New York, away from here and this"—he looked for the word and found it—"devastation."

His word did its job, sending pictures of Barrington through my mind. The closed factory. The boarded-up stores. Jonah Wright born with a hole in his heart and no insurance. The Bordens living in a house with a roof like a sieve. Brooke Frazier, impregnated by a rapist she wouldn't name.

I'd helped them. I gave them money, time, a ride to far away doctors. Small things.

If I'd been in New York, what would have happened to them?

"I need to think," I said. "Get data, like you say."

"Can I see you tomorrow night? At the playground?"

"It's still there," I confirmed.

"I'll pick you up at seven."

"No. I'll get there the way I got there the first time."

"No way. You are not—"

Because I wasn't getting into an argument about my safety in a town of people who loved me, I interrupted him with a kiss.

I'd never taken a kiss before, so I was clumsy. My focus on my objective overrode my passion. My lips were too stiff and my head pushed forward too hard, but once Chris gave up on finishing his sentence, he came to me, giving willingly what I took from him.

A simple, sweet good night kiss between two kids who had their entire lives in front of them and the weight of the world on their shoulders.

CHAPTER 28

CATHERINE

I couldn't sleep. I stayed up for hours, lying on my back, watching the moonlight shift over the ceiling mural.

Every option seemed like a possibility. Go to him. Risk everything. Undo the damage of the past thirteen years. It seemed so easy.

The other option, stay in Barrington. I'd found meaning in being needed and loved. The rewards of my efforts. Stay for the people who need me most. Let them take care of me.

As the night went on, shades of both options appeared. Tell Chris he had to stay here part time. Take Harper with us. Sell the last of everything and put it back into the community and split. Tell Chris maybe. Tell him I wanted more time.

Yes to all. Yes to some, no to some. I wasn't used to weighing so many options and internal negotiations. I didn't feel capable of handling it.

I AM A GROWN WOMAN.

THOSE FIVE WORDS came to me about two in the morning. I rolled them around in my head.

I AM A GROWN WOMAN.

I am a young woman.

I can do anything I want.

I am trapped.

I am free.

I am ashamed that people will know what he does to me.

I am a grown woman.

I am afraid to leave here.

I am afraid to stay.

I want him.

I want him.

He'll hurt me. He's hurt me already.

This is a game to him.

This is a game to him.

You'll give up everything you work for,
and for what?

> *Mommy and Daddy won't*
> *love me anymore.*

They're long gone.

> *Does he still love me?*

Do I still love him?

> *What's it like to not love him?*

I am a grown woman.
I know my own mind.
I know my own heart.
I'll do what I want.
I'll take my own risks.
I will own my own failings.

> *I'm terrified.*

I can do what I want, and he
can join me in that or not.
He's a grown man.
I don't have to love him,
not now, not ever.
I can just do what I want.

> *You're scaring me.*
> *What will I do if I am left alone again?*
> *What's going to happen to me?*

This can't happen again.
Do you understand?
This cannot happen again.

It might happen again.

You can't let it.

I can't control him.
And it might not be him to
blame in the end.
He might be offering something I don't want.

Do you blame me for being scared?
Do you blame me for wanting to run away?
What if this happens again?

I'll take care of you.

175

CHAPTER 29

CATHERINE

*M*y room went from black, gray, blue, to the yellow light of morning angling through the windows. I got up when I was too hungry to stay there.

Physically, I was a wreck. But mentally, the sunlight had brought a clarity that brought my emotions to heel. I had seen real human suffering, and I had seen people survive real pain. I was afraid of a broken heart, but what was a broken heart in the face of losing a child or going hungry?

A part of me wanted to run toward the risk, saying "bring it on," while opening my arms to whatever Chris Carmichael had in store for me. And the other part of me was very clear, very firm, and spoke in a voice years older.

It said I would not do a single thing that didn't serve me. If I made a sacrifice, it would be because that sacrifice would make me happy. If I made a demand of him, it would be because I couldn't live without the thing I was demanding.

I didn't know what any of that meant. Specifically, I didn't know what to demand, but when I came to it, I would know. I'd opened the door to my needs, and I trusted they would walk through when they needed to. I was not going to rely on Chris to figure this out for me, nor was I going to second-guess him. I was going to take him at his word, and he was going to take me at mine.

I came downstairs to find Harper at the folding table in the dining room. She was scribbling in a notebook, and I expected to see a bunch of unintelligible signs, symbols, and codes. Instead, it was her uneven script with cross-outs, arrows, and lines across sentences.

"Good morning," she said, not slowing her pencil one bit.

"What are you writing?"

"College essay."

I looked over her shoulder and saw my name. "What's the question?"

"I have to describe someone I admire." She covered her paper and continued scribbling. "Don't let it go to your head."

I put my hand on her shoulder and squeezed it. I didn't have any words of gratitude, and I knew she didn't want them anyway. "Can I make you something to eat?"

"I'm good."

"It's nice to see you not crying."

"Same for you." She put her pencil down and cracked her knuckles. "Reggie came by last night."

"He owes you an apology. Don't you dare speak to him until he apologizes to you."

"I sliced his head open with a garbage pail lid," she said incredulously.

I put my hands on my hips. "There was no excuse for him speaking to me like that in front of you. I'll get my own apology, and you'll get yours. In the meantime, I don't want him coming around here, and I don't want him to be alone with either one of us."

"Oh my God, do you think he came here alone? You

should've seen the team of assholes he was with. And I say asshole in the most affectionate way." She counted on her fingers. "Johnny. Kyle. Pat. Even Juanita came with him to make sure he didn't start calling anybody names or getting violent. It was kind of weird."

I wanted to accept his apology so that I could move on with my life, but I was still kind of mad. I surprised myself. I'd never thought I was much of a grudge holder. But maybe Chris brought that out in me.

I went to make breakfast.

"Chris called," Harper shouted from the dining room. "I left the message behind the phone."

I whipped around with the coffeepot in my hand, turning so quickly the torque almost sent coffee flying. Behind the wall phone, on a little pad we kept for such a purpose, was a note in Harper's handwriting.

Chris says he will be at the playground at 7 PM.
Doesn't want you coming in the dark.
Please drive. Or call him to pick you up.
PS - I have condoms in my nightstand. Take them if you want.

THERE WAS A NUMBER UNDERNEATH, the area code from Doverton. The club.

Reggie had apologized, and this was my town. I wasn't getting in the car and wasting gas to go a mile. I'd come and go as I pleased.

I was a grown woman.

CHAPTER 30

CHRIS

I didn't think of my efforts with the tree as a complete failure. I hadn't gotten what I wanted, which was my mouth and hands on her chest, and her promise to continue seeing me.

But I woke up feeling as if I'd gotten something. I didn't know what that was. I couldn't define it or count it. Couldn't draw a conclusion from it. But it was good, and it was enough. She'd given me the idea.

The idea couldn't be quantified or counted. I didn't have an exact string of words to describe what it was. But it involved a result, and I could build a formula from that.

Catherine would continue to be who she was. She would continue to give of herself to others. And she would be with me. All that equaled our happiness and the end of my wandering around in the wrong world.

Again, I didn't know what that meant as far as the future. She needed personal connection. She would never be one of New York's charity mavens, only partly because I wouldn't be a billionaire hedge fund manager for much longer. But after last night, I felt as if I knew her better, knew what she needed to live her life, and I was eager to provide it.

I got a text from Brian over breakfast.

— *WHAT ARE YOU DOING?* —

— *Eating eggs and toast.* —

— *In Barrington USA?* —

— *Yes* —

THE PHONE RANG. It was Brian. I'd obviously said something to piss him off. Maybe he didn't like toast.

I answered the phone and stepped outside into the rose garden that I used to tend. "What's your problem?"

"Barrington?" he snapped. "With the glass factory?"

"Yes?"

"And you don't know about the new talk over in Silicon Valley? About the Barrington factory? This is bullshit. You told me you were out, but you're just getting out to start something else. You going to just take the money and not cut me in."

"Brian, I don't know what you're talking about."

"Sure, asshole. You think I don't know you by now?"

"What's that supposed to mean?"

"Dude, you take everything and close the door behind you. That's how you operate. I never thought you'd do it with me. But you are."

"I was born and raised here. It's perfectly natural for me to show up to see the people I grew up with."

"That just makes me think you're the one who spearheaded the deal. Not cool. Not okay. And possibly a breach of contract."

I took a deep breath, then another. The fall sky was flat blue, the morning sun was shining, and I was not going to let him think I was fogging him over. "I came here to bury Lance, and I'm staying for a while. I am not here to secretly team up with some venture capitalists opening the fucking factory. Given the choice, I would burn the factory to the ground. I understand why you don't trust me. I understand why you think I'm going to take all of the money you're paying for the fund and leave. But if there's a loyal bone in my body, and there are a few, at least one of them has your name on it."

"I want in."

"There's nothing to be in on."

"There will be, my friend. If you're not stabbing me in the back, and maybe you're not, I still want in."

"Noted. But don't hold your breath."

"Noted."

We hung up, and I sat back down to breakfast. The eggs had gotten dark and translucent at the corners. The toast was chewy and cold.

Nobody trusted me. Lance had, but he'd never wanted anything from me but food and a little affection. He still gave more than he took.

I'd never betrayed Brian, but betraying him had never been in my best interests. If it had been, if some opportunity to fuck him over for my own benefit had shown itself, what would I have done?

It's business.

I would've said that. And I would've meant it. It would have been its own answer to just about any question.

Leaving my breakfast, I went back outside and called my ex-wife.

"Hello? Christopher?" People chattered in the background.

"Do you have a minute?"

"Five of them. I'm about to go into a board meeting for Montano."

The children's charity had meetings this time of year in Italy. I'd forgotten.

"This won't take long. Not if you answer honestly."

"I'm intrigued," she said in a voice laced with suspicion.

"Why did you marry me?"

"Oh, *dio mio*, Christopher. Now you ask this?"

"I married you because I thought you were as good as it got. There. I said the hurtful thing. Now you can just say what you have to."

I heard the flick of a lighter and a deep inhale. She must be in Milan. She never smoked at home. "I married you because you had potential."

"What kind of potential? Money?" I needed her to just admit it, but I knew she wouldn't. If I'd been so sure of the answer, I wouldn't have needed to call her.

"God, no. You had plenty of that, which was nice. You could have become a good man. But, you know, *que sera*."

"I didn't become a good man?"

"I don't have all my life to wait." Another long exhale.

"I thought you married me for the money."

"Of course you did. I have to go. We can talk later, okay?"

"Sure." I hung up.

If you wanted people to trust you, you had to make them money. You could be a nice guy, real prince, but if it didn't make any money, who cared? That wasn't the kind of trust I was in business for.

Some things weren't business.

My business was going to change. I just didn't know what it was changing into.

CHAPTER 31

CATHERINE

*T*he little playground behind the old trailer park was deserted. The plastic was cracked, colors faded, and cigarette butts littered the sand. I accidentally tipped over a beer can sitting on a bench meant for watchful parents.

The trailers had been removed after my father died, leaving stumps of rusted pipes. The good pipes and the copper had been ripped out long ago and sold for scrap. Electrical wires had been dug up with spades and snow shovels in the middle of the night.

I didn't know my father owned this trailer park. Not until he died and his assets became mine and Harper's. I hadn't been able to sell the land. I would've sold it for anything, but nobody wanted it.

I heard him coming. He made no move to disguise his footfalls in the leaves behind me. I turned around, resting my arm over the back of the bench as he broke the tree line, hands in pockets, trying to look harmless.

He was anything but harmless to me. His posture drove forward in a way I never saw on the men in town, alienating my mind's better judgment from my heart's desire. He divided and conquered just by smiling.

"I didn't see your car," he said as soon as he saw me.

"I walked." I turned around. It was the only way to stop myself from running into his arms.

"I don't like you walking alone at night." He came around the bench and sat next to me, flicking the empty beer can away. "This isn't a good neighborhood. Trust me, I grew up here."

I got up, picked up the can, and put it in the lone space in the cardboard six-pack that was lying a few feet away. "There are no bad neighborhoods in Barrington for me."

I sat next to him. We sat in silence for a few minutes. Maybe it was seconds. Maybe we sat for hours, each getting used to the presence of the other again.

"I wondered if you'd come," he said finally.

"Why?"

"We have a habit of temporary good-byes turning permanent."

"I wanted to tell you something."

He sat up a little straighter. It was a defensive posture. "Tell me then."

"I admire you."

A little laugh escaped his lungs. "Sure."

"You wanted something. You spent years getting it. You fought hard. I admire that. And now you're here, which is brave. And you're looking back on what you fought for and thinking you maybe made a mistake. Maybe you fought for the wrong thing. I admire that too."

He shook his head a little, as if he couldn't accept my words.

"There was this woman," he started.

A tingle of jealousy ran through me. I had no business being jealous, but did anyone?

"Before my ex-wife and after I paid capital gains for the first time, there was this woman. She was a maybe. She looked a lot like you. She was from a small town in Georgia, and she seemed as gentle as you. Of course, I didn't realize any of that right off. I didn't realize that she and you were cut from the same cloth. So I let myself care about her without putting it all together. And then this stupid thing happened. We were getting coffee and she got there before me, so she paid for herself. And I get there just as the guy is giving her change. It's a dollar and some coins. She takes the dollar, and she takes a quarter out of the coins and puts the rest of the tip jar. And I said, 'Why did you take the quarter back?' Believe me, I could've asked about the dollar, but the quarter really bugged me. She said she might need it for laundry or the parking meter. She didn't have a car. And it's not like I didn't have someone going over there to do her laundry and her chores for her. But she took the damn quarter back. Why? What kind of person won't give a quarter? Give the whole thing because they might need it for something that would never happen?" He ran his finger over his forehead. "It took me a few days to realize that I broke up with her because she wasn't like you. I mean, she really ran down my expectations. Because no matter how much they look like you or act like you... no one was going to be you."

"I was here the whole time. But I'm afraid I would have disappointed you anyway. You had me on some kind of pedestal."

"I'm here now, at the base, looking up."

"I'm a different person now."

He smirked a little, relaxing his shoulders. "You're not the girl I took up the top of that slide, but you're the culmination of her."

He leapt off of the bench and held out his hand. I took it, and he pulled me up to the play structure. We clattered up the ladder, and I found myself laughing.

The space we had occupied as young lovers was so much smaller than I remembered, and it was littered with dead leaves and human detritus. Cigarette butts, broken glass, an empty bag of chips; none of it bothered me. There was only him, with his eyes glinting in the moonlight and the fresh smell of aftershave.

His kiss was gentle and sweet, a request for more. A door he held open for me. I could walk through or I could walk away.

My arms were bent at my sides as he embraced me, running his hands down my forearms to my wrists until he lifted them and put my hands around his waist. Only then did I yield completely, tightening the coiled springs of my muscles around his body until he was as close to me as I was to him.

We kissed as though we couldn't let go, like adolescents, afraid that if we broke for a second to speak or touch we would break some kind of spell and shame or realization of the consequences would flood us and we would have to make some kind of adult choice. We kissed as though any bond between us was between our mouths. Fighting to keep our tongues together as he ran his hands over me, I wished for more. Everything. I wanted to leave him there, spent, to take every drop from him.

His hands got under my shirt, down my waistband, and still we kissed. We kissed as he reached down so far he had to bend his knees. I lifted myself onto my toes to help him get under my underwear, his finger reaching toward where my desire had collected.

I gasped so hard when he touched me that I almost stopped kissing him. That was not allowed. The kiss must be maintained. That was the rule. He knew it. He held my head to his with one hand and his fingers dug deeper, but the other reached into me.

When he broke the kiss, my first reaction was not disappointment but the fear that he was stopping, that he was breaking his bond.

He kept his mouth close to mine and said, "I want you. I've never wanted anything as much as I want you."

He kissed me again and touched my swollen nub, stroking it just a bit. My back arched like a cat's and he had to work harder to reach me. As we bent together, angling until we were kneeling before each other, kissing, his fingers flicked me as if he could read me like a book.

"Come for me, Catherine. Give it to me."

I was confused for a moment about who was giving what to whom, but I didn't have time to sort it out, because I was giving him what he wanted and I was taking what I wanted, exploding in his hand, breaking the kiss with my cries, letting it flood me so slowly, so powerfully, that I laid my entire weight on him, flying back, reaching through his jacket to scratch through his shirt.

He finished me, letting me come down gently, and pulled his hand out of my pants.

"Thank you," he said.

"I'm supposed to be thanking you."

"When we were kids, all I wanted to do was taste you." He held up his fingers. They were shiny and slick, and I was a little embarrassed by my body. He put his finger on his tongue and licked it off. I was shocked and turned on at the same time. "You've fulfilled an adolescent dream. It's as sweet as I imagined." He stuck his middle finger in his mouth and sucked it clean. I hoped this wasn't finished, because the way his lips curved around his finger made me want to experience that mouth so much more.

"Thank you."

He reveled in my shame and embarrassment, and it was exactly those things that made me want him even more. He wanted me to give him everything, and I wanted him to have it.

I was seized with fear. He would take everything from me. He would leave me a husk, a molted skin in the sun, and go away with my heart. My mother had been right—he was dangerous. Not to my standing in society, not to my finances, he was dangerous for my soul. I didn't want to be a husk. I didn't want to be left with a shell of a life.

I stood up hurriedly as if I had an appointment. I didn't know how else to act. I couldn't tell him my fear because my fear didn't have words. My fear came through my mouth, and he had already proven he owned my mouth.

A rustle came from behind the trees. The laugher of adolescents. Through the branches and trunks, flashlights bounced. Cigarette smoke stung my nostrils.

"We're about to be invaded," I said.

"We were here first." He straightened my shirt.

"Tell them that." I jumped off the play structure, landing well.

"I'll walk you." He jumped down with me as four teens broke the tree line.

I recognized Zack and Lily. The other two were in darkness. They all fell into silence. I waved. Zack waved back.

"Come on." Chris put his hand on my back and we left in the other direction, leaving the playground to the children.

CHAPTER 32

CHRIS

I could feel her arousal drying in the creases of my fingers as she sat next to me on the way-too-short drive to her house.

I knew how to seduce women. I knew I could have her on her back if not tonight, then by tomorrow. I knew that as spooked as she was, she was also turned on. My dick stretched against my pants and my balls ached for her. She might've been a little freaked out when I sucked her off my fingers, but tasting her made me want her even more.

"It looks like you need the roof redone," I said as we pulled down the long drive.

"We'll figure it out."

It had been clear from the beginning that she didn't want anything from me. I wanted to give her everything, but I also wanted to take everything.

"If you need a loan…" I shut myself up as quickly as I could, but what was said was said.

"Have I mentioned that you can go to hell?" She said it with a fine layer of the sweetest saccharin. A shell of a joke over a core of gravity.

I pulled up in front and shut the car. "You have mentioned that. But the offer stands."

I wasn't willing to hear her tell me to go to hell again, so I got out of the car and let her out. She stood near enough to me that I could smell her. The roses. I could've kissed her. I couldn't tell if she wanted me to, but I could tell that she was daring me to. And if I wanted a woman and she dared me to take action on wanting her, I usually took her up on it. There had never been a reason not to take what was given freely.

Instead, I walked toward the door, and she fell astride me. She glanced at the top floor.

"Do you think Harper's waiting for her sandwich?" I asked.

"She never asks for one, but she always eats it."

Two moths banged around the porch light, slapping their bodies against the hot glass. Now was the time for good night kisses and final gropes.

"How long are you staying?" she asked, looking at my car.

"As long as it takes." I took her by the chin and turned her face toward me. "As long as it takes." I stepped back and opened the screen door for her.

She didn't get out her keys but turned the knob and opened the front door. "Good night, Chris."

"Good night, Catherine. And thank you."

She opened her mouth to say something, but she closed it and nodded instead. She gently closed the door and I was left on the porch, watching the screen door slap shut.

I sat in the car in her driveway for too long. I couldn't move. A woman like that? A woman like that would stay beside you through lawsuits. A woman like that would wait for you while you were in jail, and she'd send letters every day. A woman like that would stand behind a man who was fucked up, using all the strength in her body to hold him straight. A woman like that forgave a sinner.

You could take everything from a woman like that. You could steal her heart, take her money, give her a life of sincerely-made broken promises.

A man could love a woman like that to death.

A man could love a woman like that forever.

A man could stand by a woman like that and watch her bloom.

Water her.

Tend her gently.

Respect the thorns. Love the rose.

A man could walk beside a woman like that the rest of his life.

I'd been at a crossroads in her front yard before. I'd made choices based on adolescent priorities, and now I felt that crossroad again. There was no tomorrow. There was no later, no taking it slow. I had now. I'd waited long enough.

The tennis ball I'd collected at the club was on the floor of the car, the yellow reduced to deep mustard in the shadows.

I grabbed it, got out of the car, and looked up at her room.

Her lights were on.

CHAPTER 33

CATHERINE

*T*he crumb-dusted plate by the sink told me Harper didn't need a sandwich. I shut the light and went upstairs, dragging dissatisfaction behind me.

What did I want? More Chris, but how? Did I want him now or wish for the past? Did I want the broken man or the beautiful boy? Did I want him now? Later? Or never? Would the reality of him break the world I'd built for myself?

I walked right by the master suite. I didn't want to sleep under Reggie's mural. Didn't want to see it or feel its weight over me. I went to the front bedroom and flicked on the light. The bed was still made, and next to it sat the boxes of unread letters. The mattress creaked when I sat on it, and the cardboard flaps coughed dust when I pulled them up.

A parallel universe sat in a crumbling pile. A universe where I'd gotten the messages and bent my life around Chris Carmichael. A universe where I was a different woman, maybe happy, maybe miserable, maybe some shade in between. But in every iteration, I was different.

I picked up the top letter and opened the flap. The glue had hardened long ago, and the letter inside was brown at the fold.

I didn't want to be different. If I'd found the first letter or the last, I would have been a different Catherine. I liked who I was. I hadn't thought about it until I closed the envelope flap, but I'd done much with little. That alone was worth the price of every other possible outcome.

Pock.

I dropped the envelope, freezing at the memory of that sound.

Pock. Pock.

I threw open the sash and leaned out the window. Chris was in the front yard, tossing the tennis ball and catching it in one hand. The beautiful boy was purely a man, and though I was different, I was not immune to him.

"I need to talk to you," he said, tossing the ball up at the window.

I surprised myself and caught it. "Wait for me." I slapped the window closed before he had a chance to answer.

When I got out the front door, he was waiting. I took his hand, put my fingers to my lips, and jerked my thumb upward, toward Harper's room. I pulled him to the backyard, and he put his arm around me.

He pulled me closer as we walked. Strong. Secure. As real as the day we met, the thrill of his presence and his touch vibrated throughout my body. I was glad he was there because I could barely walk, but he was the reason I felt as though the earth was dissolving under my feet.

I'd intended to bring him behind the headstone where he'd left me, but the stone, and all the others around it, was covered in burned-out branches. I couldn't recreate the moment for him or myself. I stopped at the white fence. "I…"

I couldn't finish, because the realization hit me like a cyclone that started in my heart and twisted through my mind. The scene of my past was blocked by the fires of my present.

"What is it, Catherine?"

"It's not the same."

He nodded, and I knew he wasn't stalling. He nodded because he understood me. Maybe I never knew if he was having exactly the same thought.

I tore my eyes away from the web of bushes and looked the man in the face. "We're different. Things that happened, we've done things. And they changed us. We can't go back. We don't get a redo."

"But we have now."

"What if I don't love you now?"

"Are you saying you don't?"

"I'm saying I don't know."

"I think you will."

"You filled a space for me. What if I don't have that space anymore? What if it's all filled up already?"

He touched my face with a tenderness that melted the skin underneath it. I wanted him, but I didn't need him.

"Chris—" My voice broke. "What if now isn't enough?"

"My now wants your now. Come forward with me. All you've done in this world has made you the woman that would have been too much for the Chris you knew. Back then, I needed simple answers, and you gave me one. That answer, money, it isn't the answer anymore."

I put my hand on his chest and bit my lip against giving him an easy response. We both deserved better.

"It's not simple anymore, is it? Back then, you gave me reason to be my own woman, and when you left, I became that woman. I don't have any simple answers now." I felt his heart beating through his jacket. Felt the life in him fighting to get out. I wanted to see that life. "I don't know if I love you, but I want to know the man you are and I want to see the man you'll become." My tears got cold in my eyes, and I blinked them away. They weren't tears of disappointment, despair, or tension. They were tears of relief. "That's not the same as it was, is it?"

He wiped a tear away with his thumb. "It's not the same. We won't know until we try. I'm not going to ask if you still want me. You can't still want that kid. But do you want me now? Because the man I am now wants the woman that you are now."

I barely had a voice to answer, so I whispered, "Yes."

His kiss was as tender as his touch, gently greeting my lips. The greeting turned into something warmer, then hotter, as his tongue broke past my teeth, touching mine, connecting us at the mouth in a way our hands could not. I clutched his jacket, his hair, wanting to know his body as well as I knew my own.

He pushed against me, hip to hip, hitching me against him until my legs were wrapped around his waist. He carried me up the back porch. Still kissing, I reached for the doorknob and opened it. We were locked together through the house, up the stairs, and I directed him to the room at the end of the hall. The room with the made bed and the boxes of old letters. Groping him, kissing whatever piece of skin I could find, I tasted the present and the unknown future.

When he closed the door, the hall light cut off. Moonlight streamed through the windows. We undressed each other like animals getting past our prey's skin, reaching for the vital organs.

I'd never felt this before. I'd wound my entire emotional life into despair and unworthiness, and suddenly they were coins flipped to passion and desire. His body was firm and powerful and my body was melting into liquid fire, bubbling at the edge of the pot, lid tapping and rattling.

Laying me on the bed, he said, "You are more beautiful than I ever imagined."

He dropped his pants, and his erection was a singular perfection. Finally, I'd have it again. He crawled on the bed and drew his hand down my body, between my breasts, over my belly. I felt as though I'd never been touched before. Not by him. Not by this man. My body answered his hand by arching, my blood answered by closing the gap between us.

I gasped for him, saying, "Yes. Now," without making the words.

"I want you right now," he whispered with a voice as thick as the darkness. "And I'm going to have you, but I'm not rushing. We both waited too long."

"I have all night."

"Good," he sighed into my breast, kissing around the base, working his way to the peak.

He sucked until it was hard. I squirmed, but he took his time, doing the same to the opposite side. His lips worshipped my belly and hips, my thighs and my knees. He pulled them apart and ran his tongue along the inside of one, then the other. My fingers were woven through his hair, gripping tight when he got close to my center.

He paused with his mouth so close to my core I felt his breath on my wet skin. I held my own breath until my lungs hurt. My exhale was a whimper. His voice was the rustle of the grass in the wind. My name was a prayer.

His lips were reverent, soft, slow. His tongue ran slowly along my seam, not just offering pleasure but tasting me, as if the pleasure wasn't mine but his. When it reached my clit, the darkness behind my eyelids lit up with lightning and my ears rushed with my own cries. The pot bubbled over, hissing against hot metal.

And still, he was slow and deliberate. My legs opened wide for him, and my body bent and thrust with an orgasm that rushed hard and fast after thirteen years of waiting. Lifting my hips off the bed, I twisted, and he grabbed me by the thighs so he could keep his face between my legs as I flipped.

"You have to stop," I lied, pushing myself onto his face and coming again. I fell back, away from him. "Oh, my. My God."

Resting his weight on one elbow, he smiled at me with a slicked face. "I wouldn't have known how to do that when I was sixteen."

I climbed on top of him, straddling his shaft as it lay against the length of my seam. "I can't wait to find out what else you know."

"This." He shifted my hips forward then back, sliding against me.

I followed his rhythm, aroused all over again. I bent and kissed him. "Can you come like this?"

"I want to fuck you."

Sitting straight, I rode him, taking control of the pace. "You're thinking about protection."

"Yes."

"I just finished my period."

"Kismet."

I whispered in his ear. "I also got a condom from Harper."

We laughed, and I reached into the nightstand drawer. We put it on.

Lifting myself a little, I gave him room to guide himself to my entrance. I placed my weight down slowly, letting him into me, feeling my body react to his presence.

We were joined again, but this time it was without fear, without sneaking. We weren't two romantic kids against the world, but two people. No more. No less.

He pushed his body against mine, letting me set the rhythm and wrapping himself around me when I leaned into him. My lips, his lips. My heart. His heart. One breath. One moment inside of a life.

My orgasm blossomed like a rose, opening from a tight bud into a splay of petals and pleasure. I cried into his neck, and he thrust hard into me twice, then sucked in a breath, knotting his brows and arching his neck to look me in the face as he filled me.

This was what he sounded like when he came.

This was what he looked like now.

It was beautiful.

CHAPTER 34

CHRIS

*W*hen I woke, the sky was just turning chambray on the eastern horizon. Catherine was wrapped in my arms, her body rising and falling. A long strand of light brown hair lay across her cheek and over her eyes. I pulled it away and tucked it back with the rest of her curls so that I could see her face in the sunrise.

I disentangled myself to go to the bathroom, still naked and aware of Harper's footfalls in the hallway on the other side of the door. As I swung my legs over the bed, my foot hit a dusty, desiccated cardboard box. The flaps weren't sealed or puzzle-locked. I had a feeling I knew what was inside before I even peered in. From above, in the dim light, it looked like a box of garbage, but it didn't take long to see the angled seams of envelopes.

My letters.

I'd written them. I bought the paper, the pens, paid for postage. I'd licked the envelope flaps with my spit after dumping all of my heart's desires onto the pages. And yet I didn't feel like I had the right to look inside. They were Catherine's property. My heart, on a page, delivered to her. A moment in time that I thought was my own was now her possession.

When I got out of the bathroom, she was roused a little, half sitting up but still so drowsy that her body was limp.

"Good morning," I said, getting on the bed with her.

"Good morning." She put her arms around my neck. "I hate to bring this up, but I haven't really thought about it. And I think I have to."

I knew what she was going to say before she even said it. "I'm a free man. I could be somewhere else, but I don't have to be and I don't want to be."

"No one is in New York waiting for you?"

I kissed her. "They'll send out a search party at some point. Did you ever want to go to New York?"

She didn't exactly push me away, but she didn't get closer either. "I can't just run off to New York." She smiled, and a little laugh escaped her throat. "That's ridiculous. I can do whatever I want. People still need me here, but they won't for long. I was thinking, just a week ago, that I can go anywhere and do anything. I was going to go to London. The places I've never been. And I don't know why I'm hesitating with you."

She was so honest with herself and with me. I could love this woman if I only knew who she was. And I was sure—positive— that she would love me too.

"We have a gap," I said. "A big gap to fill where our lives have been. We have to string ourselves across it."

"Christopher Carmichael, I didn't know you were such a lyrical man."

"Didn't I talk some shit about flying monkeys?"

"You were a poet in the making."

"Then let me grind these rusty gears back to life."

She shifted to her side, propping herself on her elbow. "I'm ready."

I knew what I wanted to say, but not how to say it. No matter what I came up with, it was something I'd heard before or was too small in scope. I wanted to draw around us with permanent marker and show her the beauty of everything inside the line.

"We were destined. I don't want to make the mistake of saying that there's a now us and a future us. We were always in the stars, and for the past thirteen years, we were just waiting for the planets to catch up."

"That's not bad for a hedge fund manager."

"I'm not a hedge fund manager anymore."

"Really? What are you?"

"Yours."

CHAPTER 35

CATHERINE

*T*he counter was too crowded. I couldn't fit a Dixie cup between the pots and bowls. Mrs. Boden arrived. She was over ninety and wore bangles on her wrists every day of the week.

"I can take two." She held out both her hands. I put a bowl in each.

"You got it?" I asked.

Behind me, the screen door slapped. It was Reggie, still bandaged.

"I have it, young lady," Mrs. Boden said before going out.

I should have been nervous to be alone with him, but I'd known him so long, I couldn't find fear. "Reggie, good morning."

"Morning." He jammed a hand in his jeans. "I brought the truck so I could take the big stuff." With his free hand, he indicated the food everyone had dropped off for the soup kitchen.

"I can give you a hand."

"I'm sorry," he blurted. "I called you a lie, and I knew it was a lie, but I said it anyway."

"Okay."

"And I had no business getting in your face. My feelings are the same, but I have to be a man. Just be a man about it. You're a woman of your own mind. That's the end of it. We've been friends for a long time and that's all I want from you if that's what you have to give. I'm upside down thinking I spoiled that."

I picked up the heaviest stock pot, and he rushed to relieve me.

"Thank you."

He turned and kicked open the screen door.

"Reggie."

He stopped with the door half open.

"Things are changing and you sensed that. You reacted to it. You didn't spoil it. We're still friends, but like I said… things are changing."

"Yeah."

"But not what I think of you. That hasn't changed. We're still friends."

"I appreciate that. I couldn't live with myself."

I put my hand on his arm and gave it a gentle squeeze. "You'd better get that out or everything's going to be cold."

As he walked across the back porch and I went to the kitchen to get another pot, Harper barreled down the stairs in her yellow polo.

"You're working?" I asked. "I haven't made you lunch."

"Don't worry. I got it." She yanked the plastic tail of the bread bag off the top of the fridge, spinning it in the air before catching it.

Mrs. Boden came back in. "Got room for two more." She cradled two bowls in her arms and headed out.

Harper leaned into the pantry for a jar of peanut butter.

"Are you all right?" I asked my sister.

"Fine." She snapped a shopping bag from under the sink and dropped the jar of peanut butter and loaf of bread into it. She tried to leave, but I put my hand on the door. "What?"

"You're not fine."

"I'm going to be unfine and late." I knew the warehouse shifts as well as she did, and she wasn't late. When she realized I wasn't budging, her shoulders slumped. "I'm as fine as I need to be."

"Taylor?"

"That's over. He needs to have his life. I'm not going to hold him back."

"That's awfully mature of you," I said through a haze of disbelief.

"Whatever."

I took my hand off the door and wedged myself between her and it. "How are the college applications going?"

She shrugged. "I don't see the point."

Reggie clopped up the porch to get more pots, and I pulled Harper into a corner to give him room.

"What's that supposed to mean?"

"It's, like, a hundred dollars per application."

"How many do you want to send out?"

"Three. Stanford. MIT. Michigan."

I would give it to her even if three hundred dollars meant I had to stay. "You have to become what you were meant to be."

"Oh, give me a break."

"Harper." I put my hands on her biceps. "I never thought I was meant for anything. I wasn't pretty like Marsha. I wasn't smart like you. Mom always dreamed so small for us. But she was wrong. I was wrong. I became something here. I found my purpose in my people. But you? You're never going to be your best self here."

She looked away from me, twisting her mouth into a defiant curve.

"Maybe," I added, "you'll find your purpose and Taylor at the same time."

"We're all going to find Taylor." She clopped the floor between her feet. "There's talk he's buying the factory."

"Our factory?" I exploded from the inside out. "That's wonderful news! We haven't heard a thing since... was he the one we cleaned it for?"

"No. It's..." She shook her head. "It's complicated. But it's real and you know what? I don't want to be here when he's here."

Behind her, Johnny and Pat joined the march of food-carriers.

"Do you have three hundred dollars?" My offer was tinged with hope.

She looked less thrilled. "It's three seventy-five, and I can put it together."

"Are you sure?"

"If you let me get to work already."

I hugged her first, planting a long kiss on her cheek. "I love you, Harper."

"I love you too."

She pulled away and brushed past Reggie to get out the door.

CHAPTER 36

CATHERINE

*T*he soup kitchen closed at two. We cleaned up, distributing the pots and bowls back to their owners, and went home. I didn't repeat Harper's news and wouldn't until I knew for sure. But in that time, as I chatted with my people, exchanging smiles and hugs, I realized I wasn't needed anymore. I didn't know whether to feel free or lonely.

Chris's rental car was in the front yard. Inside, the dining room sconces glowed and a beat-up wooden table stretched from entry to egress. He sat in one of the plastic folding chairs from the back porch.

"Hi," I said, dropping my bag by a table leg. It had been scratched to the raw wood by an army of cats. "This is… big."

"Biggest I could find."

We stepped toward each other as if we were molding the space between us.

"I'll bite. Why does size matter so much?"

Fingertips touching. Palms pressed flat together. Bodies against each other.

"We have a lot of stories to tell and I don't want to run out of space."

I glanced at the tabletop. A hundred rings marred the wood, but there wasn't a story on it that I could see.

With my head turned, he laid his lips against my cheek and kissed it, breathing deeply. "You smell like paprika."

"I need to wash up."

"I'll go with you."

"Tell me what the table's for first."

"It's the distance between who we were and who we are."

"No wonder it's so big."

In one smooth motion, he picked me up, then carried me upstairs. We didn't make it to the bathroom. By the time we were at the top of the stairs, we were kissing as if we wanted to eat each other alive, clawing our way to each other's skin.

Half-dressed, he propped me against the wall outside my bedroom and peeled off my pants. I unbuckled and unzipped him, feeling the throb and heat of his arousal in my fist. I'd never imagined how much I'd want it, and I'd never imagined I'd ever feel so empowered to take it. My boldness shocked and freed me.

Holding me up by the legs, he pushed toward me and I guided him so he could drive into me with the force of an animal. I grunted. He exhaled.

"I'm having you in the shower too."

"And on the table?" I gasped as he thrust hard.

"Table's not for that."

Angling his hips to put pressure on my clit, he took me faster. I was aroused beyond all thought, but it was hard to concentrate against a wall.

As if reading my mind, he took my hand from his shoulder and guided it between my legs. "I want to see you make yourself come."

I started to object. That would be too shameful. Too embarrassing.

"Show me," he said, deep inside me.

My reaction to his intensity wasn't in my mind or heart. My spine vibrated and I nearly came from his command.

Any thought of shame was drowned and washed away. I rubbed my clit as he fucked me, letting my orgasm wash away any idea of shame. With him, I was fully myself.

"Yes," he hissed and thrust harder, grabbing the flesh of the backs of my thighs, slowing as if savoring every thrust. He buried himself in me, pinning my hand between his body and my clit. I felt his pulsing as he filled me.

When he was done, he gathered me in arms that never seemed to get tired and carried me to the shower, where we made love again.

CHRIS PULLED our one comfortable chair in from the living room and placed it at the center of a long side of the table. His hair was slicked back and he smelled of spicy soap.

"Stay here," he said before kissing my forehead.

"Okay?"

He was already on his way up the stairs, taking them two at a time.

He wouldn't discuss where we were going or what we were doing. He had some kind of future for us on his mind, but had made it clear he wasn't interested in bringing it up yet. I was relieved, because though I wanted to discuss our future, I feared I wouldn't like the results of the conversation.

Because how could this work?

I needed to find a new life, and he already had one. He was

based in New York, and though I might travel, I didn't know if I could ever really leave Barrington.

Chris came down more slowly than he'd gone up, taking his steps carefully, looking around the three boxes stacked in his arms.

The boxes of his letters.

He placed them on the table and pushed the stack to the center. "Our story is here."

"Oh, Chris. Didn't you see? I'm so sorry, but most of them are impossible to read."

He slid off the top box. It landed on the table in a poof of dust. "I'm here to fill in the gaps." He opened the box and grabbed a handful of envelopes. "Upper left corner is the day I left. Bottom right is the seven hundred and forty-nine dollar check. We'll go horizontally. If I calculated it right, we should have enough space for all the letters folded into thirds."

"I don't get it. You want to…"

"Lay it all out. My entire story." He plucked a letter off the top of the pile and took out the paper. It was water damaged and all the ink had run. "This is on letterhead." He flipped the envelope over so he could see the postmark. "Right. So it goes about…" His eyes flicked from one edge of the table to the other. "Here." He laid it two thirds of the way to the right, letter tucked under the envelope flap.

I picked the next one off the pile. The postmark had crumbled away. I slid the letter out, unfolding it. Letterhead again.

"'—time I moved to Park Avenue.'" I read what hadn't been washed away. "'—aller than I'd like for Lance, but zip—'" I scanned to the bottom, where a few more words had survived.

"Zip code matters," he said. "I had a place on the Lower East Side that was fine. All the roommates moved out and I just took over the lease. But Brian, my partner, was pretty adamant that I was always going to be a second-rate player below Fourteenth." He shook his head as if getting the dust off. "Street. Fourteenth Street runs east-west. There's below it, where the creatives live, and above it. He said I needed to have a Park Avenue address, even if it was big as a closet."

"How big was it?"

"It had a two-burner stove and a sink as big as that postage stamp." He took the envelope and laid it next to the first letter. "But I had Lance, even if he was miserable in that tiny studio."

"How could you tell?"

"He shit in my favorite shoes."

I laughed. He took another letter off the pile.

I grabbed his hand. "Wait."

It was my turn to take the stairs two at a time. I rushed to the hallway, threw open the closet door, and gathered up as many of my photo albums as I could carry. When I went up for my second trip, Chris helped. Soon we had them all piled at the foot of the table.

He told me the year and season of his move to Park Avenue, and I located the right photo album.

"Oh," I said, seeing which era of my life it was. I pressed my fingers against a picture of my parents and me in the town square.

"That the Labor Day Barbecue?"

"Memorial Day. Daddy stopped funding it a few years after the factory closed, but it went on without him. Bernard and his band just set up. People brought stuff."

He put his arm around my shoulder and brushed his thumb along my neck. "This is a special place."

"It is. It's a dead end, but it's home."

"It's our home."

"Yeah." The album page's plastic skin crackled when I pulled it back. The photo came right off. I put it on top of the letter it went with.

"Why isn't Harper in the picture?"

"She was at MIT."

"Wait, what?"

"She didn't finish."

"Why not?"

"It's a long story."

His arms snaked around me, turning me toward him, my body tight against his. "Catherine, I need your long stories. I need to live them with you."

"It's so much."

"It is, but we have nothing but time and a really big table."

Could we bridge the years between us? Could we understand each other? Or would the exercise make it worse? Would we see each other's bad decisions and get disgusted or ashamed?

"What if you don't like what you find out?" I said. "What if I don't live up to your expectations?"

"I have more to worry about than you." He tipped my chin up so he could look in my eyes. "Whatever we did, that makes us the people we became. And I know I loved the girl you were. I'm pretty sure I'm in love with the woman you grew into."

For a split second, he looked like the old Chris on the day we were caught in the office, face cut into stripes from the afternoon light coming through the blinders. His skin folded into Ws at the corners of his eyes and his voice had grit in the corners, but he was that same boy with that same raw love.

I wanted him to love me again, because I was sure I loved him.

"Let me make you some tea and I'll tell you what happened with Harper when Daddy got sick."

CHAPTER 37

CHRIS

I didn't have a timeline to complete the boxes of letters. Good thing, because there was no way we would have made it. That afternoon bled into the night. Harper came home, stopping to look at the boxes and the new table.

"I'll tell you some other time," Catherine said. "Have you eaten?"

She hadn't. Catherine fed her, then me, and Harper went upstairs.

"You were telling me about the subway." Catherine tapped the letter in question. Half a page of the most boring narration in the world. She sat in her chair and put her hands in her lap.

"It's a little dry. We can skip it."

"Nope."

I told her what was in the letter, as far as I could remember, expanding on it as necessary, and she told me about her life at the same time. She'd sold the paintings off the walls to bail Trudy out of jail for a DUI. She'd posted bond for half the town at some point or another.

When we realized it had gotten too dark to read my writing,

we turned on the lights, laughing at the obvious solution. Morning came and went. We ate sandwiches and drank homemade iced tea.

We were tired, but we couldn't stop. She was fascinating, creative, driven to keep the people she loved above water. The table was crisscrossed with photographs and paper scraps when we got to the point when Errol Dannon went off to college. She beamed, eyes glittering with tears.

"He was having such a hard time with math in eighth grade. He thought he was dumb, but he wasn't. And when he went to Duke, he said it was because I drove Harper to tutor him that he made it." She sniffed, wiping away a tear.

My handkerchief was damp, but I used it to wipe her eyes.

"Thanks." She shook off the sobs. "I think we should take a break."

I tipped the box. A single envelope slid along the bottom. "There's one more." I handed it to her.

"This one's in good shape," she said, flipping to the front. Her brows knit. "No postmark? No stamp?"

"Might have been stuck in another envelope?"

She shrugged and opened it. When she unfolded the page, two tickets fell out. I put my elbows on my knees, leaning as close to her as I could without crowding her.

"What is this?"

"Read it."

She met my gaze for a second, then went back to the page and read.

Dear Catherine,

This time, I'll come with you wherever you want to go.
I'll stay where you want to stay.
I am at your service from this point on.

All my love,
Christopher.

THAT WAS the shortest letter yet. She looked on the back of the crisp, white page. Blank.

She picked up the tickets and read them. "The Sistine Chapel?"

"You like paintings on the ceiling. Figured it was a good place to start."

She was still confused. "The date—"

"Enough time for me to get you an expedited passport." I reached over to wipe her eyes again, but she took the handkerchief and dabbed her eyes herself. "The tickets... it's just one thing. There's more. Paris is beautiful."

"I don't know," she squeaked.

"What don't you know?"

"They need me." She swung her hand toward the front door as if the entire population of Barrington could fit through it.

"Let them decide that."

"This is my home."

"You can still let me take you to Europe."

Her head was bent over the last letter. A teardrop fell on the paper with a heavy *tick*. She rubbed it into a gray streak.

"Catherine."

"I don't know how I feel."

"You don't have to."

She swallowed thickly. "I'm tired of crying." She sniffed, not looking up. "But I keep doing it. It's like a habit. I keep thinking everything's just going to be bad forever. And I think because if things got good, no one would need me. I wouldn't have a purpose. I'd be just..." She looked up, past me, to the ceiling, the morning light, the bare walls. "Nothing. Useless."

I gathered her hands in mine. "Your work in the world isn't done."

She tightened her fingers around mine. We sat like that for a long time. I'm not a praying man, but I prayed. For me. For her. For the possibility of an *us*.

It was her decision. I'd already made one for us. It was her turn.

The effort involved in shutting up was monumental.

Her hands loosened, but I didn't let go. I wouldn't. Not until she spoke.

"So..." She cleared her throat when the word caught, looking at me with eyes clear of sadness. "Is it cold in Rome this time of year?"

"You'll go?"

"I'd love to go. I'd love to be with you."

I leapt off the chair and held her. "Thank you," I said into her neck.

She laughed. It wasn't a reaction to something funny. No. It went on too long for that. It was a laugh I couldn't kiss through, though I tried. She laughed because she was happy, and I laughed with her.

I'd replaced her tears with laughter. I'd done much without her, and I'd done much for her. But I hadn't achieved anything until I turned her sadness into joy.

CHAPTER 38

CATHERINE

*A*ugust was hot and sticky in Rome, but somehow, with the fountains and carless plazas, it was bearable. Maybe Chris made any kind of weather seem perfect.

I looked at my watch.

"She's going to be late," Chris said. "You know Lucia's always late. It's an Italian thing."

Something strange had happened between Chris's ex-wife and me. She'd had us and a few others over for dinner the day after we arrived in Rome the first time, six months earlier. We chatted over wine and I helped her shell peas. We didn't have a single thing in common except for Chris, which should have inspired me to steer clear of her. But I didn't.

I liked her.

Apparently she liked me too. The next morning, Chris got a note at the hotel, respectfully requesting permission to be my friend. I felt as if she were asking for my hand in marriage.

"I'll tell her no," Chris had said, rooting around his pockets for a pen.

"Don't you dare!" I snapped the letter away.

"What? Why?"

"She's different than anyone I ever met before." I folded the paper and put it back into the envelope. "And she thinks I'm interesting."

"If it would make you happy…"

"You make me happy." I slipped my hands under his jacket, circling his waist. "Lucia is entertaining, and I'd like to be her friend. But if it makes you uncomfortable…"

"No, no, no. It's fine. Just don't go shopping with her."

"First, shoes! Then, bags!"

Lucia and I hadn't bought anything but wine and pastry together, and yes in the six months I'd known her, she'd always been late. You could set your watch to it.

"We have to get moving early if we want to make it to Lake Como." He tipped back a tiny cup of espresso, finishing it in a single gulp, as expected in Rome.

Across the cobblestone plaza, flower and fruit sellers had set up tables. They did brisk business in single carnations and little, sealed grey boxes. A heavy door into the side of the church was chocked open. A stream of people came in and out. Some went in holding the flowers and boxes and left without them.

"But I want to go to the catacombs," I said before finishing the last of my pizza, which was a completely different thing in Italy. Just a piece of flatbread with sauce and a dusting of cheese. A snack. "And that apartment in *Trastevere* feels like home."

"You want to stay then?" Chris reached across the table for my hand, and I gave it to him.

Behind him, as people passed on the sunlit plaza, the pigeons fluttered up in a wave, cooing and dropping back to peck between the cobblestones. He'd let his beard grow in. I loved running my fingers through it when we kissed.

Chris would go wherever I wanted. He'd show me places he knew or discover new things with me.

"Harper's coming home from Stanford for break."

We'd been traveling for two months this time. Our first trip to Italy was a week in Rome and six weeks in Tuscany. Then we went home. I took care of the Barrington house. He took care of business in New York. We were separated for two weeks, and we decided never to do that again. That was nine months ago.

"We can come back, or we can skip the *Citta Della* whatever festival in Como."

"Chee-*tah*. *Dio mio*, Christopher." Lucia's voice came from behind me.

I stood and we double-air-kissed. That had always looked phony to me, but when you actually kissed the person and touched them in some other way, it meant you liked them.

I was surprised how much I liked Lucia. I'd known Barrington and Doverton women who kept their hair and nails perfect like she did, and I knew women who put on fussy airs and cared about status. But none of them were as grounded about it as Lucia. She didn't gossip, and she didn't look down on me for my short, unpolished nails or quick ponytail. She liked that I didn't care about my social station, even as she made no excuses for the fact that she cared deeply.

"Chee-*tah*, then," Chris said, double-kissing his ex-wife, who now spent half her year in her home country.

"It's not a cat," she said, sitting next to me.

"Whatever. If I need a translator, I'll hire someone."

"You can look right in front of you."

The waiter came before she could explain. She ordered lunch in Italian, I did the same, and Chris ordered in a halting patchwork of syllables that I explained to the waiter.

"Excuse me," I called to the waiter before he left. In Italian, I asked, "What's going on over there? With the open door?"

He answered, and I thanked him.

"What was that?" Chris asked.

"It's the feast day of Saint Monica."

"From *Friends*?"

Lucia rolled her eyes and nudged me.

"They're bringing offerings," I continued. "Silly man."

"How is it that you're at your woman's mercy?" Lucia asked. "What would you do without her?"

"It was worse in Iceland."

"Everyone speaks English there," I protested.

"Two weeks." He held up two fingers. "Two. And she was talking to people. And not just ordering dinner."

"I spoke at a third-grade level and I barely had a vocabulary. Seriously. It's not a big deal."

Lucia, in typical Italian affection, put her hand over mine. "You have a gift."

"Well, whatever." I hid my face by taking a drink of water.

"No," she *tsked*, wagging her finger. "This is not to be ashamed of." The rest she said in Italian too quickly for Chris to understand. "This gift is what God gave you. And if you are ashamed of it, you are ashamed of God." She slid back into English. "God made me beautiful, and I use it."

"Indeed," Chris grumbled amicably.

"Anyway, are you going?" Lucia asked. "To Como?"

"We haven't decided," Chris replied.

"I want to see my sister."

"So you return."

"Maybe. There's a lot to see. I don't know. It's not like there's a schedule or a point." I shut myself up. I'd started to bring up my trouble with Chris. I didn't want to float around the world all the time. I loved traveling and meeting new kinds of people, but something was missing.

Lucia tapped my arm. "Come with me. *Un momento*." Then, to Chris. "We'll be back."

She led me across the plaza, not missing a step in six-inch

heels on uneven cobblestone. Her bag was tucked under her arm, a gift from her current beau.

"Where are we going?"

She stopped at one of the sellers and bought a little grey box. "To make an offering."

"What's in there?"

"Porridge. Don't look like that. It's just a little."

We passed through the doorway, into the back of the basilica. The stone floor was worn smooth, and with the sun in the side of the sky opposite the single stained glass window, the little foyer was dark.

"I told you I'm not getting married again," she said.

"Have you changed your mind?"

"No. Please. Save me from it."

Through the far entry, we entered a large nave lit with ceiling lamps. Along one side, a long table was set with candles. Celebrants slipped their carnations inside vases or laid them before the paintings of the saint and left bills and coins in gilded chests. Some prayed at a red velvet rail that ran the length of the table.

Lucia put her box with the rest, dropped cash into the box, and kneeled, tapping me to follow. "Santa Monica was Saint Augustine's mother. She followed him all over the world. Now, you can say what you like about that. But she was a mother first."

I nodded while she rested her chin on her folded hands. She was going somewhere, but I couldn't imagine a destination.

"I love children. Always. I begged to take care of my cousins. I thought I would be a mother. But God gave me a gift instead. He made it so that I had to give myself to children who didn't have someone to take care of them. I'm not marrying again, at least not soon, because my gift isn't to be a wife. Chris will vouch for that." She stood and smoothed her skirt.

I followed her to an empty pew and sat next to her.

"It has been so good to know you," she whispered.

"Thank you. You too."

"You pick up what people are saying and speak back to them in their language, but your gift isn't languages. Your gift is *listening*." She took my hands. "I'm going to make you an offer to use that gift."

"What kind of offer?"

"I need you at the Montano Foundation. It is a big organization all over the world, and it does good work. We feed children and build schools. We need someone like you, who listens and can learn a language. Who is generous. Who wants to help. Children need you."

My blood thrummed. Work. I'd never had a job. I'd always assumed I didn't have a skill worth paying for.

Lucia continued, "There will be a lot of travel, but we'll talk about it later. First, you think about it, because you won't be so free to move around when you want."

"Okay. Thank you. I'll think about it."

When we got back to the plaza, I could see the café. Our lunches were at the table, and Chris was on the phone. He invested his own money, but still loved taking risks and crunching numbers. He loved his job.

Our lives revolved around two things. My travel whims and his work.

How would a position with Montano, where I'd have to travel where and when I was needed, fit into that?

CHRIS and I were alone on a small jet flying out of a private airport outside Rome, taking up two of the eight seats. The rest were empty. We'd stayed in the apartment in *Trastevere* another week, missing the Como festival. I'd been too wound up to take the short hop to Tuscany. I spoke less, got lost in thought mid-sentence, stared out the window for too long.

I hadn't told Chris about Lucia's offer. I wanted to think about it first, but I just kept thinking.

Would I be separated from Chris for weeks? Months?

How could I ask him to prioritize my work and his at the same time?

What did the future look like if I did this?

We were in the air before he spoke. "Catherine."

"Yes?"

"When we get home, is this over?"

"What?" I was too shocked to make a whole sentence. How could he think that? What had I done?

"Just tell me."

"Wait…" I twisted in my seat to face him. He'd shaved off his beard, and his eyes were soulful and honest. Had he looked this mournful since I spoke to Lucia? How hadn't I noticed?

"I want you to be happy," he said. "But you've been saddish."

Saddish? I'd been thinking about my life, for sure. Who I was. What I wanted. He'd turned that into me wanting to leave him, and that wasn't going to work.

"Christopher Carmichael." I grabbed the front of his shirt. "You are a piece of my happiness." I tugged the fabric. "You are the love of my life. Do you hear? Do not ever imply this is over unless you want to end it."

"Then what's on your mind?"

I let go of his shirt and smoothed it down. "I wanted to think about something before I told you."

"Well, you've thought enough. We're partners. You don't get to think that much without me. Out with it."

Lucia had put the official offer in an email. I got it up on my phone and showed it to him. His expression went from mild irritation (probably with his ex-wife) to deep consideration, to a sharp nod as he handed the phone back.

"You taking it?"

"I don't know. I want to, because I'm bored. Not with you," I said quickly. "Not with you at all. Not with traveling or the new places. I love all the people. I love seeing things I never thought I would, and there are so many things I never even imagined. Northern lights. Pompeii. So much. But I'm bored with myself. I don't have a purpose. I'm not fighting for anything. It's like…"

I'm dead inside.

But that was too harsh and unfair. He'd breathed life into my heart, but there was only so much he could be for me.

"It's like you need to become the next version of yourself."

"Yes."

"And you're not going to get there globetrotting."

"Right!"

"But you're afraid you'll lose me if you have your own needs."

He'd hit the bull's-eye, and he knew it. I couldn't look at him.

He unsnapped his seatbelt, then undid mine. He looked down the aisle to the front of the plane. The attendant was tapping on her phone in the galley. He craned his neck to the back of the plane, then stood and held his hand out to me. "Come with me or I'll carry you."

I laid my fingers in his palm, and he pulled me to the sleeping quarters and snapped the door shut, cutting us off from the rest of the plane. We were alone with a tiny bed and a standing shower. He unbuttoned his shirt.

"Chris, really?"

"Really. I don't know how to make you believe me." He shrugged off his shirt and made short work of his pants. In seconds, he was as naked as the day he was born. "Do you see me?"

I took in the beauty of his naked body, but when I laid my hand on his chest, he moved it away. "I see you."

"I have nothing." His voice was cut through with resolve and hunger. "This is me with nothing. I came in this way, and I'll go out this way. This body? It has needs. I need food, water, and sleep, okay? That's how it stays alive. I have a brain. It comes with the package. It needs to work and to figure things out. If I'm not doing that, I'm dead, because it's here, in the skin. And I have a heart. When I'm naked and all the other shit is gone, it's part of me. It needs you. You."

He was making my point for me. I nodded, about to explain that I understood. He needed me and if I was doing something else, his basic needs wouldn't be cared for. But he took my shirt at the hem and pulled it over my head.

"Chris, I—"

"Give me a minute. I'm not done." He stripped me down until I was naked and vulnerable in front of him. "You come with this package." He looked at all of me as if cataloging. No lust. No lingering on the most feminine parts. "It needs food, water, sleep, shelter. Your heart needs love, and that you have covered, by me. But the mind?" He took my head in his hands and kissed my forehead. "It's been neglected long enough."

When I blinked, tears fell onto my cheeks. I swallowed hard, took a hitching breath, and tried to thank him, but I couldn't.

He went from my forehead to my temples, my cheekbones, my jaw, my chin, and hovered over my lips. "I won't allow you to die. Not any part of you."

I couldn't hold myself back. I threw my arms around his shoulders and kissed him with everything I had, and he let me. He leaned back and sat on the bed, still connected to me at the mouth. I felt his erection between us, and my entire body—with its need for food, water, and sleep—needed it. My heart, with its need for his love, needed it. My mind, with its yet undiscovered needs, needed it. I lifted myself on my knees and he guided himself into me.

"I love you, Catherine of the Roses."

"And you. I love you."

I moved against him in a rhythm that gave both of us what we needed, together.

EPILOGUE

CATHERINE

*H*e'd planned his proposal with the care and patience of a lawyer arguing before the Supreme Court. He'd had the ring, the place, and the time.

Unfortunately, my flight out of Sri Lanka had been delayed. He'd spent the first week with me, then gone back to New York. I was supposed to follow, and he was supposed to propose at the top of Freedom Tower. Instead, he'd met me at the airport, carried me upstairs half asleep, and put the ring on my finger while I was dreaming.

Of course I'd said yes. I may have been crazy busy, but I wasn't crazy.

And now, here I was under a tin ceiling painted with roses in a designer wedding gown my fiancé's ex-wife had commissioned. It was gorgeous. The veil was set in my hair with roses. My nails were done, and my lipstick softened my face.

Lucia was behind me in a pink business suit, hooking the back of the dress closed. Marsha was pinning and repinning my hair.

"I love it," I said.

"Of course you do," Lucia replied.

"Chris is going to fall in love all over again," Marsha said. "He hasn't seen you yet, has he?"

"Not for a week."

We'd been separated for that long before. We had been apart for three weeks when I was setting up a school for girls in Morocco, but this week had been the hardest. He had stayed with Johnny while I stayed at the house, planning everything with Lucia and Harper. And Taylor, of course, who'd found his way back to Harper. But that was another story entirely.

Outside, I heard kids playing and guests laughing. Everyone was coming. The entire town, the board of Montano, our friends from New York. Everyone.

There was a commotion downstairs, in the living room. Someone was calling for Father Grady. I wasn't supposed to go down. Chris had promised a surprise.

Harper banged up the stairs and threw herself into the room. Her sentence was one long word. "Cassie-the-pregnant-FBI-agent-her-water-broke-so-they-need-to-get-married."

Cassie the Pregnant FBI agent was with Keaton the Handsome Brit in the Dark Shirt from my birthday party.

"Okay?"

"She's trying to leave. She doesn't want to take the wind out of your sails."

"Nonsense." I gathered up my skirt.

"Can't they have the baby first?" Lucia objected.

"I don't know!" Harper said. "It's a thing!"

"Americans are such prudes."

Whatever the reason, it wasn't for me to judge why they felt as though they had to get married first. I flew down the stairs as a voice with an English accent floated over the confusion.

"We need rings!"

"Use ours!" I called as I was halfway down. Father Grady was putting on his stole and flipping through his book of sacraments. "Chris! Give them the rings!"

Chris spun around and put his hand over his eyes. "I'm not looking at you!"

"Who has them?" I shouted, then froze. The mantel, the wall, the entire side of the room where we were to be married was crammed with roses.

"The best man," Chris said from behind his hand. "Back upstairs, woman!"

I couldn't back away. Couldn't turn from the roses. "Chris."

Johnny came in from the back in a long-tailed tuxedo jacket and bolero tie. "I got it."

The clamor went on as people shifted and took new places. Taylor was Keaton's best friend, so he acted as best man for the moment.

"The roses," I said.

Chris had given up on not looking at me and laid his hands on the bannister. "You're beautiful."

"So many."

"Seven hundred forty and, well, we were short five. Now we're up five."

I searched his face for a moment, trying to place the need for over seven hundred roses.

"The garden's down ten though. I promised I wouldn't cut from there, but we have some helpful people around who did it anyway."

THIS IS A GUARANTEE. I pay my debts. I'm coming back with the money and more. And when I do, I'm bringing you a rose for every dollar.

"I REMEMBER."

"I kept my promise."

"You did."

"Except about the garden."

"You kept your promise, Chris." I went down the stairs, and he met me at the bottom. "You kept promises you didn't even make. You made me whole."

"You made you whole. I just watched it happen."

The impromptu ceremony ended with cheers as the groom kissed the bride. Taylor kissed Harper. Couples I barely knew kissed.

And Christopher Carmichael, the lost boy who'd become a man, the persistent letter writer, owner and friend to a puppy named for a knight, looked at my lips in their sweet pink hue and leaned in.

"No!" Harper shouted and wedged herself between us. "You waited thirteen years. You can wait another ten minutes." She pushed me up the steps. "Go go go."

"She's not even hooked in back!" Lucia shouted from the top of the stairs.

Chris kissed my hand before it slipped away. "See you in ten minutes, Catherine of the Roses."

"See you forever, Christopher Carmichael."

I went back up to my room, and under a ceiling of roses, I prepared to spend the rest of my life becoming who I was meant to be.

❀

THE END

❀

Follow me on Facebook, Twitter, Instagram, Tumblr or Pinterest.
Join my fan groups on Facebook and Goodreads.
My website is cdreiss.com

ALSO BY CD REISS

ROYALTY SERIES

King of Code | *White Knight*
Prince Charming | *Prince Roman*

HOLLYWOOD ROMANCES

Shuttergirl | *Bombshell* | *Bodyguard*

THE GAMES DUET

Marriage Games | *Separation Games*

THE CORRUPTION SERIES

Spin | *Ruin* | *Rule*

THE SUBMISSION SERIES

Submission | *Domination* | *Connection*

OTHER STANDALONES

Forbidden | *Hardball*

91R00139

Printed in Poland
by Amazon Fulfillment
Poland Sp. z o.o., Wrocław